LAST STAGE
TO ASPEN

ALLAN VAUGHAN ELSTON

SAGEBRUSH
Large Print Westerns

First published in Great Britain by The Western Book Club
First published in the United States by Lippincott

First Isis Edition
published 2019
by arrangement with
Golden West Literary Agency

A catalogue record for this book is available
from the British Library.

ISBN 978–1–78541–689–7 (pb)

Published by
F. A. Thorpe (Publishing)
Anstey, Leicestershire

Set by Words & Graphics Ltd.
Anstey, Leicestershire
Printed and bound in Great Britain by
T. J. International Ltd., Padstow, Cornwall

This book is printed on acid-free paper

34767819

To the *Little Giant of the Rockies*, champion mountain climber and bold pioneer of the Western Slope frontier — the Denver & Rio Grande Railroad

CHAPTER
ONE

Wes Brian, crack driver on the Leadville-to-Aspen run, braked his stage to a stop on the grade below Independence Pass. A bank of fir arose steeply to his right while a chasm to his left gave echoes, from far below, of cascades at the head of Roaring Fork. This was high country, only a little below timber line. When the brake was set and the six-in-hand stood gratefully still, Wes stepped to the ground and spoke to one of the coach passengers.

"How'd you like to ride up front, Miss? You could see things better."

He wasn't looking at Honora Norman but at the man beside her. His cool gaze told both the man and the girl why she was being invited to ride with the driver. The man, Jote Griffin, was a middle-aged miner who'd just sold his Leadville claim and was heading for Aspen with a walletful of cash. His mood of celebration had led him to force attentions on a young and pretty passenger.

Two others in the coach were a threadbare schoolmaster and an Aspen counter clerk. The clerk snickered. The girl smiled faintly. The schoolmaster looked stern. The miner flushed. To all four it was clear that the driver was offering not scenery but a rescue.

"Thank you." Honora stepped promptly out of the coach when Wes Brian opened its door.

He handed her up to the front boot and climbed to a place by her. Then he released the brake and snapped the lash of his whip over the lead span. "Let's go, ponies." The six horses were off at a trot, trace chains jangling, the big Concord lurching between cliff and precipice down the narrow, ledgy trail.

Unconsciously he was showing off a little. For Wesley Brian was vain of his coachmanship. Horses were his one love and handling them was his one art. He knew he was at his best with six reins in one hand and a twenty-foot coach whip in the other. Some called him Snapper Brian because he could flick the bloom off a thistle at whip's length.

The girl sat tense and breathless, her gloved hand gripping the seat rail. This was her first trip over the divide, her first wild ride down a mountain, her first touch of perilous adventure. Until today she'd never seen a man like this gray-eyed young driver, reckless yet superbly confident, alert and yet serenely relaxed. His voice came faintly over the rattle of wheels. "If I'm joltin' you too much, just sing out."

The sound of upcoming traffic made him stop at the first wide spot in the trail. A four-mule ore wagon passed them and crawled on up toward the pass. "Headin' for a smelter at Leadville," Wes explained as he drove on. "Aspen's had to team its ore out since the first strike there seven years ago, back in '80. Couple of

2

months more and she'll have a railroad or two. After that it'll be goodbye to mules and stagecoaches."

Honora knew, of course, that both the Rio Grande and the Midland were laying rails madly, racing each other to Aspen. The newspapers were full of it.

A series of sharp curves made Wes walk the horses. The girl could relax now. She glanced at the driver's windburned profile. "What will you do," she asked curiously, "when the stages stop running?"

His grin was half rueful. "That's just what I've been wonderin' myself. Drivin' a stage is about all I know."

Not much ambition, she thought, and felt oddly disappointed in him. Just six feet of brawn with reins in his hand and a gun strapped to his hip. More than likely he'd merely drift on beyond the frontier of rails and find another stage to drive.

The forest opened and gave a breath-taking panorama. Snow-capped peaks, collared with spruce and laced with aspen, reached in a jagged line down the sky like a row of majestic castles and cathedrals. Some were blunt and some were spired. One, nearer than the rest, had the profile of a woman sleeping face up. "We call her the Silver Queen," Wes Brian explained. "Aspen lies snug under her arm. Already she's coughed up thirty million in silver."

"How high are we?" Honora asked.

"We were above twelve thousand back at the pass. Must be about down to ten now. Aspen's eight."

They were in a nearly level grade of the canyon and Wes slowed down to cross a water run. A faster gait might crack an axle. The forewheels jolted across and then the rear.

Sliding gravel to the right of the trail made a crackling sound.

"Pull up, driver!" The command startled Honora. A masked horseman had appeared from the timber and was aiming a rifle. "You in the stage. Get out and line up!"

Had he been alone on the driver's seat, Wes might have risked a draw. With the girl sitting there he couldn't. The bore of the rifle was a black eye staring at him — as black as the man's horse and mask and boots. They were miner's boots, he noticed, not riding boots.

Other details struck Wes as his hands went rebelliously up. The man's voice seemed vaguely familiar.

Jote Griffin, followed by a frightened clerk and a school teacher, got out of the stage. The horseman made them line up with their backs to him. Keeping mounted, he took Griffin's wallet and gun. Griffin was the only armed passenger. All the while the masked man kept his rifle aimed at the driver.

He spurred to the forewheel and from there he snatched the revolver from Wes Brian's holster.

"Get back in," he snapped to the passengers. As they scrambled into the coach the bandit backed his mount about five yards from the forewheel. Not once did his aim waver from a bead on the driver's head.

"Drive on!" he commanded.

4

He'd robbed only Griffin. He hadn't touched mail and express pouches. Why? Wes could think of three good reasons. First, maybe the man knew in advance that Griffin had sold his claim and was travelling to Aspen with the cash. Second, a teacher, a clerk, a stage driver and a young girl wouldn't be likely to carry fat purses. Last, time lost in taking mail and express would make a risk, since another ore wagon might come along at any minute.

"Drive on!" the masked man repeated.

Wes gathered the reins in one hand and took the whip in the other. An idea tempted him. The whip was twenty feet long and the man was only fifteen feet away. Why not snap the whip at the man instead of at the lead span? With his rifle in command and the victims disarmed, the bandit wouldn't expect it. He'd expect them to drive frantically on. Why not snap the whip so that its last five feet would coil about the man's neck? A jerk would then unsaddle him. It was a trick Wes Brian had practised many times on a post or sapling.

The lash flashed back — as though to crack over the team. Instead its tip flicked like a snake toward the masked man's neck.

Only a forward lunge of the off wheel horse caused a miss. The tip of the lash touched the bandit's left ear and drew blood. The coach lurched forward as the man fired. Wes felt his hat jump, heard a gasp from Honora.

His arm went around her to keep her from falling off the stage.

"Are you hurt?" she asked faintly.

"Only my feelings." His free arm held her tightly as the coach swayed on.

Looking back he saw the masked man wheel his horse and disappear into the trees.

Unmounted and unarmed, a chase would be stupid and futile. So Wes kept his team at top speed down the trail. Honora recovered her composure and slipped out of his arm. She stared at the bullet hole through his hat. "He might have killed you! How far is it to . . ."

"We've got one more change station," Wes broke in. They'd changed horses four times since leaving Leadville at daybreak.

The next change was at Deane's Camp, in a canyon dell called the Grottos. Wes drew up there with his animals blowing hard.

A quick report to the station man. Then two hostlers saddled mounts and were off to the scene of the holdup.

While stage horses were being changed, the school teacher tore a page from his notebook. He jotted down a description and handed it to Wes Brian. "This is the way I remember him. Do you agree?"

Wes read it aloud to the others. "Tall, lean man on black horse; black mask; corduroy jacket and pants; black hat with limp brim; miner's boots stained with clay."

"Your whip touched his ear," Honora remembered.

"And drew blood," Wes said. He added six words to the memo: "tiny fresh cut on left ear."

No one could think of anything else and Wes put the scrap of paper in his shirt pocket. The station man rearmed him. When the fresh horses were traced up, Wes handed Honora back to the front boot. Presently they were rattling down the last lap to Aspen.

In the coach, Jote Griffin complained bitterly about the loss of his wallet.

"I'm lucky the guy didn't grab mine too," Wes grinned. "My whole lifetime savings is in it." The grin was sardonic, since his total fortune was only three hundred dollars — four months pay as a driver on the J C Carson stage line.

"You should keep it in a bank," Honora said. "Or invest it. Which reminds me, did you ever hear of a silver mine called the *Little Lucy?*"

He shook his head, giving her a curious look. Had someone unloaded a chunk of worthless mining stock on this girl? When a claim failed to hit pay rock a common practise was to incorporate it and sell shares to innocent easterners. Many of the Aspen mines were bonanzas, but a few were duds.

"Have you always lived out here?" the girl asked.

"I was born in a covered wagon," Wes told her, "on the way from Missouri to Gregory's Gulch. That was the first gold camp in Colorado."

"Then your father was a miner?"

"No. He was a Methodist preacher."

"Oh! So that's why he named you Wesley!"

Wes gave her a half-shy smile. "You guessed it. My full name's John Wesley Brian."

The canyon became a valley as they neared Aspen. It was nightfall and lights dotted the town. Lights from street lamps and saloons and from torches moving up

7

and down the mountain. Shifts were changing, men lighting their way to and from work. Sparks and black smoke belched from the tall, dark stacks of a smelter.

"Roughest part of the road," Wes chuckled as the stage bumped down Cooper Avenue between high, board walks. Chug holes gutted the street. Beer smells and horse smells came from the saloons and livery barns. Honora Norman's sensitive blue-eyed face, under reddish curls and a ribboned bonnet, wore a dismayed look. Every other shop seemed to be a saloon. An exception was the Delmonico Restaurant with soft violin music coming from it. From other doors came the sounds of tin-panny pianos and coarse laughter. A drunk was kicked out on the walk. A policeman shook his billy at two off-bounds women. "Get back on the Row, you biddies, before I run you in!"

The look on Honora's face made Wes reassure her. "This is not our best street. There's some right nice folks in this town. It's been growin' too fast, that's all. You'll like it at the Clarendon."

At the corner of Cooper and Mill he stopped at the courthouse hitchrack. Deputy Sheriff Gavitt came out and Wes gave him a report, describing the bandit by reading from the memorandum in his shirt pocket. Jote Griffin got out, demanding instant pursuit. Postal and express clerks came up and took charge of the pouches.

The Clarendon Hotel was only a block south and Wes dropped Honora off there. It was a three-storey frame with thirty rooms, the best in Aspen. The girl waved a goodbye as a boy carried her bag in.

8

Wes had a preoccupied look as he drove on to the stage barn. There Ed Blake, the agent, met him with bad news. "Sorry, Wes. Dick Page went sick on us and it leaves us short of drivers. Means we've got to shoot you out again tomorrow."

Wes grimaced. The stage to Leadville left at six A.M. and he usually got a day's rest between trips.

"Serves you right," the hostler said as he untraced the horses, "fer lettin' that bird hold you up. Lucky he didn't grab your poke, Snapper." The news had spread quickly from the courthouse.

The preoccupied look was still on Wes Brian's face as he walked toward his Hyman Street rooming house. Words of Honora Norman came back to him. "You should keep it in a bank. Or invest it." She'd spoken lightly, but he knew it was true.

Now it was after nightfall and both banks were closed. But a light showed at Frank Bayard's office on Galena Street. Bayard, a broker in mining stocks, was just about the busiest man in town and he often worked late.

On an impulse Wes turned in there, finding Bayard alone at his desk. Ore samples lay about and in one corner stood a heavy steel safe. A blackboard covered one wall and on it were chalked the latest quotations on stock of the more active mining companies. Bayard cocked a surprised eyebrow as Wes dropped three hundred dollars in bills on the desk.

"It's all I got, Frank. Invest it for me."

Bayard gave him a searching look, then smiled. He was a big golden man, still under forty, with wavy yellow hair parted in the middle. If he wasn't quite the handsomest man in Aspen he was certainly the best dressed. His massive watch chain spanned a tweed vest which had been tailored in London. "Who is she, Wes?" he asked slyly.

"What do you mean, who is she?"

The broker's smile widened. "You're a type, Wes. Cowboys and stage drivers are all alike. A hip pocket wallet is all the bank they need till something makes them start thinking about settling down and getting ahead. They never start thinking like that till they bump into a pretty girl."

"No such thing." Wes reddened a little. "I got held up today and it could happen again."

Frank Bayard counted the money. "Chicken feed," he said dryly. "What do you want to take — a short shot or a long shot? I can get you three shares of a blue chip; or thirty thousand shares of some dead cat at a penny a share."

By a blue chip he meant one of the bonanzas like the *Spar* or the *Molly Gibson*. And by a dead cat he meant a played-out claim. Yet Wes couldn't forget that more than one dead cat had upon second look become a bonanza. Like the fabulous *Emma*, once considered worthless, and which during the past year had produced a million dollars in silver.

"I got a weakness for long shots," Wes admitted. "But use your own judgment, Frank. I won't gripe if you make a bad pick." Frank Bayard gave him a receipt and put the money in his safe.

10

CHAPTER
TWO

Two pistol shots awakened Wes. He heard shouting in the street. Town Marshal McEvoy seemed to be arresting somebody. Maybe it had to do with the stage holdup.

So Wes dressed hurriedly and went out. He'd slept only a few hours and it was still no later than midnight. A man with a bloody head was struggling in the arms of McEvoy. Another was being handcuffed by Constable Sutton.

"What happened?"

A bystander thumbed toward the Buckhorn Saloon. "Gus Gleason got conked with a bottle. He runs a bar and a faro game up at Ashcroft."

"Who conked him?"

"Mart Davis. Mart lost his roll one time up at Gleason's place. Claims it's a brace layout. Swore he'd make Gleason hard to catch if he ever found him in Aspen. Tonight he did. Broke a bottle over Gleason's head."

Another bystander chuckled. "So Gleason chased him out and cut loose with a gun. Mighty poor shootin', I call it. Missed him twice."

The officers marched Gleason and Davis off to jail. They'd each draw a fine, probably. It hadn't been worth getting up for.

But now that he was up, Wes didn't feel sleepy. He wondered if the sheriff's crew had picked up a lead on the stage robbery.

A good way to find out was to drop in at the Abbey bar. The Abbey was the town's most popular saloon, always a hub for the very latest news or gossip. "If we don't know it, it ain't happened," was a boast of the Abbey's head bartender.

Even at midnight Wes found two white-coated barmen on duty there. No sawdust dump, the Abbey. Its bar was polished rosewood and its brass gleamed under the sparkle of crystal chandeliers. In Aspen, only the Brick, the Branch, or the Clarendon bar itself, could compare with it.

Most of the customers were miners. A few were gamblers and still fewer were stockmen from down the valley. None of the miners was armed. And tonight they were in a playful mood. As Wes ordered a short beer he watched a bit of hazing. The boys were teasing a down-and-outer known as the "Major," an habitual drunkard who'd become a favorite butt for jokes around Aspen. This wasn't the first time Wes had seen them baiting him, at one saloon or another. And the Major always stood for it so long as they kept plying him with drinks. In spite of his rags and blotched skin the Major always managed a dignity of sorts. Always his beard and his wavy white hair were neatly combed. No one could doubt that he had schooling and a military

12

background. Yet the baiting always ended with the Major passing out on the barroom floor.

The leading prankster tonight, Wes noted, was Charley Barrow. Barrow was a Britisher with a wine-colored face. He admitted freely that he'd been expelled from Oxford and was being paid a monthly remittance to stay out of England.

A man at a poker table caught Wes Brian's eye. Myron Lockwood! Sight of him puzzled Wes a little. Less than thirty hours ago he'd seen Lockwood riding down Harrison Street in Leadville.

It was sixty-six miles to Leadville. To get here from there you'd have to come by stage or saddle. The stage made it between dawn and summertime dark, but only by changing horses every ten miles. It would take a hard forced ride for a man to come by saddle, across a twelve thousand foot pass, between two midnights.

And why hadn't the stage passed him, or been passed by him, on the road? Lockwood's narrow, good-looking face had tired lines in it. Strange that he'd sit in a poker game after a ride like that! Something oddly unnatural, Wes thought, about the way he wore his hat. It was slanted steeply to the left.

After puzzling over it idly, Wes brushed it from his mind. Myron Lockwood was a man of high connections. He was close to the councils of the New York financier, Joshua B. Wilbur, who was here in Aspen to promote a railroad, a smelter, a new hotel and a big mining merger. Rumour had it that Lockwood was as good as engaged to the New Yorker's daughter Phyllis. Wes had often seen them out together. The

13

worst you could say about Lockwood was that he was an opportunist, a handsome, devil-may-care man-about-Aspen with an eye out for Number One. He might have a dozen good reasons for a fast ride to and from Leadville.

"There he goes! Out like a light!" The voice veered Wes Brian's attention back to the bar. He was in time to see the Major pass out cold.

"He broke his own record tonight," Charley Barrow chortled. "Fourteen jiggers. I counted 'em. Fetch him along, lads."

Ready hands picked up the Major and carried him to the street. Apparently Barrow had cooked up something special. Curious, Wes followed them outside.

He saw them lay the Major in the bed of a spring wagon. Charley Barrow climbed to the seat and drove off, his voice raised in a dirgelike song. Cheering, guffawing men followed afoot. Perhaps they were merely hauling the Major to whatever alley hovel he used for sleeping quarters these days.

To make sure they didn't hurt the man, Wes trailed along himself. The wagon creaked east along Cooper, then turned uphill to a cemetery. There two of the pranksters took spades and began digging a shallow grave. Wes wasn't really alarmed. Surely they wouldn't go too far. To see that they didn't, he mingled with the crowd and watched.

When the grave was two feet deep they laid the drunken man face-up in it. Then the spaders covered him with a thin layer of dirt, leaving only his head and neck exposed.

"He won't know nothin' about it," a miner chuckled, "till he wakes up in the mornin'."

"We must put up an epitaph," Barrow insisted. "Who's got a scrap of paper?"

His cronies delved for something to write on.

"Will this do?" Wes Brian took a scrap from his shirt pocket and offered it. His thought was to break the party up as soon as possible. When the prank played itself out they'd go back to the Abbey for another round. Then Wes could uncover the Major and put him to bed somewhere.

"Just the thing." Charley Barrow took the slip Wes offered and scribbled an epitaph on it. In the dark Wes couldn't see what he was writing. It was sure to be something ridiculous and derisive.

Barrow gleefully impaled it on a stick and set the stick upright in loose earth at the foot of the grave.

"Next one's on me," he announced. There was a rush for the spring wagon. Only a few could get on it. The others followed noisily as Barrow drove back to Cooper Avenue.

Wes followed a dozen steps, then stopped. In the gloom no one noticed him. When they were out of hearing he'd undo what they'd done.

West Aspen Mountain arose sharply above him, its top profiled like a sleeping woman, its slope aglitter with lights. A rumble up there was ore being dumped from a tram. A dozen rhythmic throbs came from as many shaft pumps.

Below lay the town itself, its decent half asleep, its sporting half shamelessly carousing. The vice houses and most of the bars stayed open all night; for the mines ran round-the-clock shifts and workers were abroad at all hours.

Wes thought of the girl he'd brought in on the stage. What would she think of Aspen by this time tomorrow? And why was she here?

Kneeling by the grave he scraped the loose earth from the derelict's chest and arms. Only his legs were covered now. He was breathing regularly, though soddenly, and there'd been no bodily injury. The starlight even seemed kind to his white-bearded face. Since hitting the skids he must have known other beds as hard as this one. A feeling of pity came to Wes. Yet there was really no great hurry to move this old soak. He might as well sleep it off here as anywhere else.

His battered hat lay by the grave and Wes picked it up. He was about to set it back on the Major's head when he thought suddenly of another hat. The hat of a poker player slanted steeply to the left. A man who'd ridden, that very day, over the pass from Leadville!

A hat slanted steeply to the left would hide a damaged left ear!

The thought jolted Wes. Myron Lockwood! Lockwood was hand-in-glove with the bigwigs of Aspen. So why would he hold up a stage?

The idea was fantastic and Wes didn't really believe it. Yet it jerked his mind away from the Major and fastened it on one question. Was there, or was there not, a tiny fresh cut on Lockwood's left ear? A cut nicked by the lash of a whip?

He must find out before Lockwood quit the game and went to bed.

Yet as he hurried back to the Abbey saloon, the logic of the point seemed to defeat itself. If Lockwood wanted to hide a nicked ear, he wouldn't play poker at a public bar. He'd keep out of sight in his room.

Other points popped and jangled. The black horse ridden by the bandit wasn't Lockwood's. The man's clothes and boots didn't match Lockwood's. Myron Lockwood rode a big sorrel and thirty hours ago he'd ridden down a Leadville street on it. And even suppose he'd known that a stage passenger would have three thousand in cash, it was hardly reasonable that a man of Lockwood's connections would go after it with a gun.

When Wes got to the Abbey the poker game was still going on. But Lockwood wasn't in it.

"He left here about ten minutes ago," a player told Wes. "Didn't sit in long. Not more'n half an hour."

Wes went out, turned west along Cooper. Next to the Abbey was the Aspen *Times*, dark and quiet now. Across from the *Times* was the Brick Saloon, a spot hardly less popular than the Abbey. Sight of it stopped Wes. His thoughts churned and a vague idea took shape.

Crossing to the Brick he found that it, too, had a poker game going on.

"Has Myron Lockwood been around tonight?"

The dealer nodded. "He sat in with us 'bout an hour ago. But not for long."

17

Wes went around the corner to the Branch saloon, on Galena. The same question got the same answer. Lockwood had played poker at the Branch tonight, briefly.

The idea was more than vague now. Wes put himself in the bandit's place. *I hit town with Griffin's money on me. If I'm accused and searched, what will I say? I'll say I sat in a few games and was lucky.*

It was even sounder than that, Wes reasoned. There was a bare chance that Griffin could describe his lost bills. But after three poker games they wouldn't be the same bills. Lockwood would lose some and win others. With some he'd buy chips and when he cashed in he wouldn't get the same bills back.

Was that why he'd played half an hour tonight in each of the town's three most respectable barrooms?

Wes walked fast and grimly to the Clarendon Hotel. The real test would be a whip-cut on the left ear.

Only Night Clerk Neal Hutton was in the Clarendon lobby. "Mr. Lockwood? He just went up to bed. Room 26."

Room 26 showed a light at the transom. Wes knocked.

"Yes? Who is it?" Lockwood's voice didn't seem worried.

"It's Wes Brian, the stage driver."

For half a minute, only silence. Then the door opened. Lockwood stood there in pants and undershirt, a tall, dark man with a narrow, clean-shaven face. His smile seemed impatient rather than forced. "Can't it

18

wait till tomorrow? I'm half in bed." He seemed perfectly sure of himself, and only slightly annoyed.

Wes looked at his left ear. A tiny cut there was still red.

Lockwood stood blocking the doorway, a hand over his mouth to stifle a yawn. Wes waited to be invited in, but wasn't.

"You heard about me getting held up today, I guess. It's all over town."

"Yes, I heard," Lockwood admitted. "Came over the same trail myself, 'bout an hour later."

"That's what I wanted to see you about. Did you pass a man on a black horse, anywhere? Wore corduroys and miner's boots."

"Might have. I don't remember." Lockwood's tone grew edgy and he half closed the door.

Wes fixed a stare on the cut left ear and asked carelessly, "Did you cut yourself shavin'?"

The answer was prompt enough to have been prepared. "No. Took a short cut through the brush and a thorn scratched me."

"The man on the black horse," Wes said, "probably cut through the brush too. But that's not where he got his ear scratched. He got it from a whip. The whip drew blood and it won't heal for a couple of days yet. If you see him, let me know."

"See him?" Caution crept into Lockwood's voice. His eyes fixed on the crown of his caller's tall hat with a bullet hole through it. "Is this a riddle? Where the devil would I see him?"

"Over that way, maybe." Wes thumbed toward the right wall of the room.

Lockwood's head jerked that way and he found himself staring into a mirror. In it he saw himself and the flush which spread upward from his jaw line to a scratched left ear.

When he whirled back to the doorway, Wes Brian was gone.

I know and he knows I know, Wes thought as he hurried down the stairs.

He got to the street and walked toward his Hyman Street rooming house. The Major, sleeping off a debauch in a cemetery trench, was completely crowded from his mind. *He won't miss me next time*, Wes thought as he hurried on. *He'll shoot to kill because he knows I know*.

Wes climbed wearily to his room and went to bed. It was more than an hour after midnight and his rest was short.

At six A.M. the lash of his whip cracked again as he drove a stagecoach east out of Aspen.

CHAPTER
THREE

Honora slept late but got down to the dining room before it closed. The waitress gave her a small table by a window. Many were at breakfast and talk hummed. Outside, carriages and hacks rattled along Mill Street and the hitchracks were full. An ore-laden mule train came down the hill and the boots of miners clumped on the board walks.

It was a new and exciting country to Honora. And in many ways less crude than she'd expected. This high-ceilinged dining room was cool and clean, its linen crisply white. Many of the breakfasters wouldn't have been misplaced in a first class New York restaurant.

At the next table a pretty young blonde was taking coffee with a tall dark man she called Myron. Myron had a tired, troubled look, Honora thought, but there was something distinguished about him. The blonde girl laughed. "Dad should be back by noon. I'll have a pillow ready for him to sit on. He's not used to riding horseback, you know."

"Took some Detroit investors up to Tourtelotte Park, didn't he, on that merger deal?" Myron waved to a man at the next table. "Hello, Frank."

Honora's eyes veered to Frank and saw a big golden man whose wavy, center-parted hair was as neatly even as his mustache. He had the air of an oracle and lesser men at his table hung on his words. "Keep your eye on the *Molly Gibson*," Frank was telling them. "The wire silver over there fairly crackles under your feet. Don't sell the *Smuggler* short, either. Those stocks'll hit sky, soon as the railroads get here."

"Which do you think'll get here first, Frank? The Midland or the D & R G?"

"Both claim they'll be running trains into Aspen by October. Looks like a dead heat . . ." The golden man suddenly broke off as his eyes chanced to meet Honora's. His gaze carried open admiration.

The Clarendon's hostess, Mrs. McLaughlin, stopped at Honora's table for a pleasant word. "Everything all right?"

"Quite all right. Thanks."

"Is there anything I can do for you, my dear?"

Honora hesitated, then repeated a question she'd asked of the desk clerk last night. "Do you know where I can find a Mr. Roger Norman?"

The hostess thought a moment, then shook her head. "I can't remember the name. So many people come to Aspen. I'll look through our old registry books. Meantime you might ask a cabby. These hack drivers are likely to know everybody."

When she finished breakfast Honora went out to the Durant Street walk. A two-horse hack waited for trade. The driver had a small round face, wise and bearded.

"Where to, Miss?" He hopped down and opened the cab door.

"I don't exactly know," Honora said. "Perhaps you can help me. I'm looking for my father. He's Major Roger Norman."

The hackman gave her a puzzled stare, then shook his head. "A major, huh? Nope. Couldn't be that one," he muttered. "Only major I know is a . . ." He checked himself and looked closely at the girl's features. "When did you see him last, lady?"

"It's been five years. He resigned his army commission and came west to Leadville. About a year ago he moved on to Aspen."

The hackman seemed relieved. "Then he must be a miner. They's an old bum around here they call the Major. Never heard any other name fer him. But he's no miner and never was."

"At Leadville my father was a bookkeeper. I don't think he ever found a position here in Aspen. He didn't write often. His last letter made me think he was sick in some way; so I came right out."

Relief left the hackman's face and uneasiness replaced it. "He wouldn't have a knife scar down his right cheek, would he?"

"A sabre scar," Honora corrected. "He got it at Gettysburg before I was born."

The hackman's mouth hung open. "Gosh, Miss! A sabre scar! He don't shave very often but when he does you can see it there. He's your old man, all right. But I sure wish you'd asked somebody else."

"Then he *is* sick?" Honora exclaimed in alarm. "Is he in a hospital? Take me to him, please."

"He ain't in a hospital." The hackman was wretched and evasive. "Fact is I don't know just where you'd find him. Right now, I mean. I know where he was at daybreak; but he's likely gone from there by now."

"Gone from where? I *must* know."

With a sigh the hackman gave up. "You want the truth, Miss?"

"Of course I want the truth."

"Well, I guess you'd find it out anyway. Last night some of the boys got playful. They rounded up a spring wagon and . . ."

Honora listened, shocked, the blood draining from her face. Then it rushed back in a flood of fury as she got into the cab. "Take me there at once," she commanded.

As the cab rattled up Durant, bits of Roger Norman's past came back to Honora and much of it tended to confirm this shameful ending. A taste for liquor had always been his weakness. It had led to his resignation from the army under pressure. Yet just after the death of Honora's mother he'd reformed briefly. After putting Honora in a St. Louis boarding school he'd gone west to make a fresh start. For four years he'd held a job of sorts, in Leadville. The relapse must have come during this last year at Aspen. Yet his first letter from here had been cheerful, almost gay; in it he'd enclosed a present for his daughter's twentieth birthday. It was a title giving her a one-fourth interest in a mine called the *Little Lucy*. Probably worthless, since no dividend had ever come from it.

When the hack stopped, she saw rows of graves. Some had marble headposts and some had wooden crosses. "Just like I thought," the hackman said. "He's gone. The sun in his eyes must've woke him up."

Anger surged back into Honora as she got out of the cab. They'd stopped by a shallow trench with freshly spaded dirt around it. A stick at one end had a scrap of paper. Honora took it and read an epitaph scribbled there.

Tears burned her eyes as she looked up. "Take me to the police," she demanded, "and I'll swear out a warrant. Who are they? I want their names, every one of them. The brutes! Treating a sick, helpless man like that!" Her face blazed. "It's assault, kidnapping, malicious cruelty . . . I won't rest till they're all in jail."

The hackman looked doubtful. "As to who they are, I can't say, Miss. A dozen or more, I heard. The night barman at the Abbey likely knows. But he ain't the kind who'd tell."

"Wait!" Honora exclaimed. "I know who the ringleader is! He's the stage driver who brought me to Aspen." She'd turned the epitaph scrap over to look at its other side. Here was the description of yesterday's bandit written by the schoolmaster and last seen in the driver's shirt pocket.

"It was sure a dirty trick," the hackman admitted, "treatin' the Major like that. But I don't reckon the boys meant any harm by it." Dubiously he drove her to the city jail.

On the way Honora read the epitaph again. She recognized it as a verse from "The Burial of Sir John Moore" with only two words changed.

No useless coffin enclosed his breast,
Nor in sheet nor in shroud we wound him;
But he lay like a *toper* taking his rest
With his *ragged* robes around him.

She wondered how a stage driver could know those lines. Yet why not? The piece was in McGuffey's Fifth Reader. Anyone who'd gotten as far as the Fifth grade could know it.

"I'll make him sorry!" Honora vowed savagely as she got out at the jail. "Him and every brute who helped him."

Marshal McEvoy and Officer Webb listened gravely to her complaint. Both were sympathetic. "We'll find your father all right," the marshal promised. "I'll put every man I've got on it and we'll scour the town. But look, Miss Norman. I wouldn't prosecute those clowns if I were you. They went too far, sure, but they didn't mean any harm."

"Just clean fun!" Honora exclaimed acidly. "Very well; if you won't arrest them I'll engage a special prosecutor. We'll let a jury decide if it's legal to bury a man alive." She turned to the hackman. "Who's the best lawyer in town?"

"Jim Downing, I reckon. Office in the Durand Block."

"Take me to him, please." Honora got back into the hack and was driven away.

McEvoy and Webb stood gawking after her. "She's not foolin'," Webb said. "We better get busy, chief. That boys-will-be-boys line of yours didn't go over."

"It sure didn't," the marshal agreed uncomfortably. "Pick up the Major quick as you can. He'll show up at one of the free lunch bars about noontime. Give him a bath and deliver him to the girl at the Clarendon. With a clean shirt on. Maybe she'll be cooled off by then."

Webb didn't think so. "Not with that red hair of hers, she won't."

Frank Bayard, leading investment broker of Aspen, had just opened his office when John Hostetter came in. Hostetter's knobby, powder-pitted face had a discouraged look. "I'm pullin' out, Frank," he announced, "soon as I can sell my claim."

"What's the matter? Your assays getting thin."

"The last dozen of 'em," the miner said, "have only run about fifteen ounces per ton. Costs that much to dig it and haul it to a smelter. Best I can do is break even. So why fool around with it any longer? I'd rather try my luck over around Telluride."

Bayard nodded. It was an old story. Some got rich and some beat the skin off their knuckles all for nothing. "Your claim's the *Lost Friend,*" he remembered. "You incorporated it for fifty thousand shares and sold twenty thousand to get operating capital. Have you still got the other thirty thousand shares?"

When Hostetter answered by laying a thirty thousand share certificate on the desk, the broker looked up his record of recent quotations.

"The last bid on *Lost Friend* stock," he said, "was a penny a share. If you dump it you can't hope for more than that, John. It would come to just three hundred dollars."

"I'll take it, Frank. Anything to get away from here and get started somewhere else."

"A stage skinner named Wesley Brian was in yesterday," Bayard told him. "He left three hundred dollars for me to invest and he said he likes long shots." The big golden man smiled. "I can't think of any longer shot than the *Lost Friend*."

"Fetch him in," Hostetter said, "and we'll close the deal."

"He just left for Leadville with his stage. Won't be back for three days. But he told me to use my judgment." Frank Bayard handed a quill pen to the customer. "Just endorse the certificate to Wesley Brian, John, and sign your name at the bottom."

Hostetter promptly made the endorsement, transferring thirty thousand shares of *Lost Friend* stock to Wesley Brian. Bayard opened his safe, taking out the money Brian had left with him. He gave it to Hostetter, who handed back thirty dollars for commission.

The broker locked the certificate in his safe. "When are you leaving, John?"

"Right now." Hostetter got briskly to his feet. "I figure to make Ashcroft by suppertime and go on over Taylor Pass tomorrow. Thanks, Frank."

CHAPTER
FOUR

At noon the two most personable men in Aspen sat at the Clarendon's lobby window waiting for the return of Joshua B. Wilbur and party from Tourtelotte Park. In financial circles Joshua Wilbur was a name to conjure with. His decision on the proposed merger up there was sure to affect mining stocks. Nearly all the Park claims were blue chips. They'd go even higher with the Wilbur interests back of them.

And Frank Bayard never overlooked a bet. It was his business to know, and to know before anyone else, just what was cooking around Aspen.

The other waiting man, Myron Lockwood, had a much more personal reason for waylaying the New Yorker the minute he stepped from the saddle. Lockwood's eyes fixed anxiously on the street and his attention strayed from the bland talk of Frank Bayard. The broker was relaying some choice gossip which had just hit the streets. About a notorious town drunk who'd been brought to a room at the Clarendon, where he lay between clean sheets for the first time in years; and where he was being coddled by a pretty young relative who'd turned up from St. Louis.

"Seems some of our barroom cutups had a little fun last night," Bayard chuckled. "This morning the girl wanted to prosecute but Jim Downing talked her out of it. Then she wanted to take her father east on the next stage; but the sheriff says she can't do it till after the tenth of next month."

"Why can't she?" Lockwood inquired absently. His mind was still nervously on Joshua B. Wilbur and on a twenty-five hundred dollar check in Wilbur's wallet. That check must be redeemed with cash before Wilbur found out it was no good. In the poker game four nights ago four Kings had looked unbeatable and so Lockwood had scribbled the check and tossed it boldly into a pot. Only to have his prospective father-in-law gather it in with four Aces.

"She can't take that old soak away from here before the tenth," Bayard explained, "because the Jenner trial comes up on that date. Seems the Major was the only eye-witness when Jenner stuck up the Fashion saloon and killed the bartender. Plenty of people saw Jenner make off down the street — but only the Major saw the actual shooting. They can't convict without him. So the girl can't take him east until . . ."

Lockwood missed the rest of it. Mention of the girl reddened the back of his neck; she was on the stage he'd held up. Desperate to redeem a hot check before Phyllis' father tried to put it through a bank, he'd rushed off to Leadville to borrow money. His Leadville connections had turned him down; but he'd learned about Jote Griffin selling a claim for cash and reserving passage on the stage to Aspen.

30

Bayard chattered on. "If she's that cute redhead I saw at breakfast, I wouldn't mind meeting her. Glad I wasn't at the Abbey bar last night. She's mad as a hornet and wants every one of those jokers boiled in oil."

"Does she know who they are?"

"Only one, so far. That stage skinner, Wes Brian." Again the broker chuckled. "He's lucky to be off on his run."

The name again fixed Lockwood's mind on his personal hazards. He'd left Leadville long before daylight, well ahead of the stage. No thought of holding it up had occurred to him until he'd stopped to water his horse at a prospector's shack just this side of the pass. The prospector was away at work but the shack had old clothes and boots and a deer rifle — with a black horse in a pen back of it. So Lockwood had helped himself to an outfit. After the holdup he'd changed back to his own mount, turning the black horse loose and hiding the borrowed outfit in a brush pile.

Everything was safe now — except for a whip-cut on his ear and a faked check. Wes Brian knew it was a whip-nick but he couldn't prove it. The faked check would wreck his chances with Phyllis Wilbur — unless bought back quickly with Griffin's cash. Then . . .

"Here they come!" Bayard announced. He went out to the Durant Street sidewalk, blond and hearty, ready to meet Aspen's most important guest.

But Myron Lockwood was there first. Bayard smiled at Lockwood's eagerness. Being something of a fortune hunter himself, he could read Lockwood like a printed page. There were three ways to get money; you could earn it; you could steal it; you could marry it. The third way, for a charmer like Myron Lockwood, would be easiest and quickest.

Joshua B. Wilbur dismounted, tired and stiff. On the walk Bayard stood chatting with one of the Detroit investors and from the corner of his eye he saw Lockwood pass a fat envelope to Wilbur. "I might as well pick up that check, while I think of it, Mr. Wilbur. The one I spent on four Kings."

As the financier looked surprised, Lockwood explained glibly. "It's on the First National of Leadville and it just happens I want to keep that account in four figures right now. Got a deal on over there. So if you don't mind . . ."

Wilbur shrugged, accepted an envelope full of currency, took a check from his wallet and gave it to Lockwood. It seemed to Bayard that Lockwood, as he tore the check into bits, heaved a sigh of relief. Then he lost interest as one of the Detroit men told about the merger.

"It's not going through. Mr. Wilbur decided against it."

Bayard arched an eyebrow. "Why?"

"Search me." The Detroit man shrugged. "Maybe it was that bit of careless bookkeeping we ran into up at the *Best Friend*. Mr. Wilbur always shies at anything like that."

Bayard could scarcely believe it. A rich mine like the *Best Friend* didn't need to pad its records. Its owners were strictly on the level. The *Best Friend* lay between the *Bob Ingersoll* and the famous *Camp Bird*, up in the Park, and all three had produced fortunes in silver.

"Nothing crooked," the Detroit man amended. "Just careless."

"Careless?"

"We looked up assay reports at the *Best Friend*. A recent one showed that a sample delivered to the chemist on August ninth assayed eight hundred ounces of silver per ton."

"So what?" Bayard queried. "Lots of *Best Friend* samples have assayed that high."

"True. But the entry was careless just the same. For after a check we found that no sample from the *Best Friend* had been sent in on August ninth. The assayer must've got his sample sacks mixed. He must have assayed ore from some other mine and sent the report up to the *Best Friend* . . ."

Frank Bayard was more than alert now. "What other mine?"

The Detroit man didn't know. The others were calling and he followed them into the Clarendon dining room.

Alone on the walk, an idea jolted Bayard. Aspen had five assayers and he knew that Luke McCoy was the one patronized by the *Best Friend*. Luke was honest as daylight. But he was human and could make a mistake. So could his yard man who handled the incoming samples. John Hostetter of the *Lost Friend* also had been a client of McCoy's. If a sample were dropped there after dark, the yard man might store it in the wrong bin. Could an assay of *Lost Friend* ore have been reported on to the *Best Friend?*

The bare possibility made Bayard set off briskly for the McCoy yard on South Monarch.

He found the assayer with a dazed, beaten look. The man listened to Bayard's question and nodded. "Looks like I'm *Nobody's Friend*, from here on. The *Best Friend* super was just in and chewed me out. When he got that report he took it in stride, because he'd had others like it. But now it makes him look bad as a bookkeeper. And Johnny Hostetter, who dug that August ninth sample, never saw the report at all."

"Why didn't he come in to ask for it?"

"He did come in, late yesterday. But he didn't mention a date. He just asked me, 'Was that last sample of mine any better than the others?' I looked in the book and said, 'About the same, Johnny. Fourteen ounces per ton.' I was looking at the last *Lost Friend* entry in my book, which was for a July assay. If you see Johnny, send him in and I'll tell him he's rich."

Bayard felt his blood pounding. An eight hundred ounce sample could spell millions. A bonanza like the *Emma* or the *Molly Gibson!* The man who owned this new one was a stage driver at this very moment whip-snapping a six-in-hand to Leadville.

But Wes Brian didn't know his luck — yet. He knew only that he'd left three hundred dollars to be invested in a long shot.

Need he ever know? Only two men could tell him; his broker and John Hostetter. Hostetter knew because he'd filled in Wesley Brian's name on the certificate.

34

But a name could be changed! Hostetter was off for the Telluride wilderness and might never be heard from again.

Temptation whispered and Frank Bayard snatched at his chance. "You're too late, Luke. Hostetter sold out this morning and left the country."

The chemist gaped. "Sold out? Who to?"

Bayard's smile was half apologetic. "To me, Luke. He asked me to take it off his hands as a favor. And I did."

In his Galena Street office Bayard closed and locked the door. He drew the window shades before turning on a light. Mid-afternoon traffic wheeled by and boots thumped on the walk. A customer rattled the doorknob but Bayard didn't answer.

He took brandy from a cabinet and poured a drink. Excitement etched crimson lines on his face. What would it mean to own three-fifths of a bonanza? It would put him in a class with Gillespie and Butler and D R C Brown! Millionaires all. They and many others had drawn fortunes from the silver lining of Aspen Mountain.

Again a customer shook the doorknob but the broker didn't let him in. Instead he opened the safe and took out a certificate endorsed by John Hostetter. The signature and date needn't be changed. Only the name of the assignee. He'd substitute his own name and no one could challenge him but Hostetter himself. Ink was hard to erase but it could be done with patience.

Should he do it now? It would be safer to wait a few days. He must give Hostetter time to get further from

Aspen. And he'd better confirm the *Lost Friend* strike by assaying another sample. It might be only a freak pocket. No use stealing a million dollars until you were sure it was there.

But the stage driver Wes Brian could be disposed of right now. Bayard did it by writing Brian's name on an envelope. He took three hundred dollars from his wallet, put it in the envelope and locked it in the safe. "I haven't invested it yet," he'd tell Brian. "What about thirty shares of *Legal Tender*, in Ophir Gulch? It's quoted at ten bucks a share."

Brian could say yes or no. Or he could have his money back. It made no difference to Bayard.

Only Hostetter could make a difference. In faraway Telluride he might read an oddity in the mining news. About the luck of Frank Bayard at Aspen. "They got the name wrong," he'd say. "It's Brian, not Bayard." After that some nosey newspaper might smell fraud and demand an investigation.

The risk of it brought goose flesh to Bayard's neck. He downed another brandy.

Again came a knock. A light, timid knock this time. Bayard mopped his glistening face, raised the window blinds and opened the door.

The girl had reddish curls and a tense, resolute face. Bayard remembered her at once. She was the pretty stranger he'd admired at breakfast.

"Mr. Bayard?"

"At your service." The broker's mellow professional smile always showed him at his best. He ushered the caller to a chair by his desk.

"I'm Honora Norman of St. Louis," she told him. "I'd only planned on being here a few days but I'm afraid it will be much longer. Till after the tenth of September." The blueness of her eyes and the exquisite oval of her face cast a spell over Bayard. He was hardly aware of it when she laid a paper on his desk. "I'll need money, so I asked the hotel to recommend a broker. They suggested I consult you. Tell me, Mr. Bayard, is the *Little Lucy* mine worth anything?"

He came out of his trance and picked up the paper. It was a title in Honora Norman's name to a one-quarter interest in the *Little Lucy*.

After scanning the endorsements the whole picture was clear to Bayard. He nodded slowly. "I think so, Miss Norman. Not much, but something. Do you know the history of this property?"

She didn't, so he gave it to her briefly. "It's up Hunter Creek, at the west toe of Smuggler Mountain. It's not a corporation but a co-partnership. Four men owned equal shares and worked it together. The ore is low grade but they made a living out of it. One partner, Clyde Waring, quarreled with the other three. He claimed they caroused in town while he did all the work. About a year ago he blew up and quit them. He said as he passed through town he'd give his share to the first . . ."

Bayard stopped himself just in time. He wanted to cultivate this young lovely. In no case must he hurt her feelings. She was already badly bruised.

". . . to the first bum I see on the street; then you'll be four of a kind." Those had been Waring's parting words to his partners.

"He said he'd give his share to a friend," Bayard amended smoothly. "Evidently the friend was Roger Norman. Yes, I think I can get you something for it. A few hundred perhaps. Perhaps even a thousand. As the railroads get nearer, those marginal claims look more attractive."

Honora smiled gratefully and stood up. "Thank you. I'll be at the Clarendon if you find a buyer."

"I'll try the three partners first. They're still on the property and may want a full title. Meantime anything I can do to serve you, please let me know." Bayard escorted her to the sidewalk and offered to call a cab.

"But of course not. It's only three blocks. You've been awfully kind, Mr. Bayard."

He stood looking after her as she moved off up Galena. A girl like that, he thought, was the one thing needed to fill his life. All he'd ever wanted were two prizes — wealth and beauty. Today he'd found both. One was already locked in his safe and the other had walked through his doorway.

He kept his eyes on Honora's trim figure till it was out of sight. Then he stepped back into his office to pick up the title paper she'd left with him. A purely speculative value but he could probably get some small offer.

As he opened the safe to put it away his eye fell upon a fat envelope with a name on it. Wesley Brian. Brian had given him carte blanche to invest three hundred dollars. Why not pass the money along to Honora Norman and have her endorse her title to Brian?

But no, that would close the deal too quickly. He must prolong it. That way he could see the girl daily and talk about it. Too, she might not appreciate his digging up Brian as a buyer. Brian was one of the cutups who'd hazed her father.

For the moment, Bayard put the *Little Lucy* paper in a separate pigeonhole and locked the safe.

CHAPTER
FIVE

At dark that evening, beyond the divide, Wes Brian trotted his stage team into Leadville. The same bullet-punctured hat was on his head and his lips had a tired droop. He whirled his outfit up Harrison Street and left it at the J C Carson barn.

The schedule allowed him a thirty-six hour rest and most of it was over before word of a new strike at Aspen came in. A speculator looked him up at the Tabor House. "What's this about the *Lost Friend*, driver?"

Wes had never heard of such a property. "You mean the *Best Friend*, don't you?"

"Nope, I mean the *Lost Friend*. They say she's turned into a humdinger."

Wes shrugged. "It happens all the time, over at Aspen. You're poor today and rich tomorrow."

"Some Leadville people own forty percent of her," the speculator said. "They're sending a mining engineer over for a look. He'll likely be on your stage."

Wes yawned. "Okay. I'll try not to jolt him out. Any word on the holdup?"

The speculator wasn't interested in holdups. But just before stage time in the morning the Leadville sheriff came up with a report on it.

"Stop at Langstaff's in Independence, driver. They want you to identify a black horse."

"The holdup horse?"

"Maybe. Miner named Fink reported clothes and a rifle missing from his shack; and a black horse lifted from his corral. Fink's in the clear himself; two men were helping him sink a shaft that day. Yesterday they found the black horse grazing loose."

"I'll take a look at it, sheriff." In the dim dawnlight Wes pulled on his gloves and moved toward the waiting stage.

Passengers were boarding it. One of them, a clean-cut young man wearing puttees and a leather jacket, might be the mining engineer. Another was an overdressed female on the move from Leadville's vice row to Aspen's.

Two other passengers, thickset and gunslung, were enough alike to be brothers.

Wes felt a nudge from the Leadville sheriff. "Better tell McEvoy to keep an eye on 'em. They're Gil and Fred Dillon and I'm plenty glad to get rid of 'em."

"What've they done?"

"Nothing, here. But they killed a man at Alma last year. At Fair Play and Buena Vista they've got hell-raisin' records a mile long. Used to run with Alf Jenner."

Jenner, Wes remembered, was awaiting trial for murder at Aspen. Was that why the Dillons were heading that way? Maybe they'd try to break Jenner out of jail. "I'll tip McEvoy," Wes promised.

In a few minutes he was rattling his stage down State Street, a glow from the smelters mingling with the light of a new day. At this same hour, three mornings ago, Honora Norman had been his passenger. All through that long day he'd been absorbedly aware of her. His ears had been alert for every word from the coach — her delight at sight of wild flowers along the trail, her awe at the majesty of the snow-crowned divide ahead. She'd wondered how they could get over it. And then, after a few fresh sallies from Griffin, he'd invited her to share the top seat.

Today her company inside would have been much worse.

From State Street he turned west through California Gulch and at Malta he veered south again. The slag dumps and shacks petered out, giving way to the tangy freshness of high country timber. The first change station was Twin Lakes and Wes made it with the sun still only two hours high.

He was off again with fresh horses. From here the grade ran up Lake Creek. But there'd be nothing steep this side of Mountain Boy Park. A fir forest hemmed the trail with Mount Massive looming almost dead ahead, its blunt, snowy crest flush against the clouds. Wes listened idly as voices drifted from the coach. Gil Dillon told a raw story but the woman didn't laugh at it. Wes heard not a word from her all day. Women of her trade, in public, generally kept on their best behavior.

Four hours out of Leadville Wes drew up at his second change station, a roadside tavern known as

Everett's. The Dillon brothers got out to stretch their legs. "When do we make Aspen?" Gil inquired.

"After nightfall," Wes told him. "It's a thirteen hour run."

"Can't you shade that a little, fella? That's a helluva long time to do sixty-six miles."

"And a helluva high pass to go over," Wes retorted. "No, I can't shade it a little. I've been late getting into Aspen, often enough. But I've never been ahead of time yet."

Gil Dillon muttered aside with his brother, then got back into the stage. Wes wondered what was their hurry. They weren't business men. The Aspen dives would still be open, whether the stage got there on time or not.

Six fresh horses were hitched and Wes drove on to Mountain Boy Park. Dick Hodge ran the station there, called the Halfway House. New horses were traced and the stage began its pull to the pass.

Wes settled his team to a plodding walk. Any faster gait would wind the animals. He heard an impatient mutter from Gil Dillon. "A snail could beat this, Fred! Why don't he get a move on?"

The road steepened, wheels bumping over rocks. Then Wes noticed that the off horse of his lead span was limping. He stopped, jumped to the ground and went forward for a look.

The limping horse was a young gray. An examination told Wes that the gray's foreleg, just above the hoof, was bruised and beginning to swell. The horse must have kicked or stumbled over some rock in the trail.

Wes called back apologetically to his passengers. "Sorry, folks. A horse went lame on me and we got to go back to Hodge's. We can hitch on another one there."

By luck this was one of the rare spots on the grade where there was room to turn around. Wes gave the gray a pat on the nose. "We'll take it slow and easy, boy. It's downhill and you won't have to pull any." He gripped the bridlebits of the lead span to lead them in an arc and turn the stage around.

Gil Dillon's truculent voice stopped him. "Hold on, kid. You can change at the next regular stop." Both the Dillons had come forward from the coach and were blocking Wes Brian's path. "Yeh," Fred echoed, "if we turn back it'd make us two-three hours late."

The next change station was at Independence, just beyond the crest of the pass. "That gray ain't hurt bad," Gil said. "Anyway he's only a horse."

Wes held his tongue, weighing the chances. There was barely room to turn the outfit around. To do it he must keep both hands on the bridlebits and walk backward in a sharply confined half circle. Wes was armed with a gun, but so were the Dillons.

"Get goin', kid," Gil said querulously. "We've fooled away enough time already. It's only six miles to the pass."

"They're steep miles," Wes said, not hoping to convince them but merely stalling for time. From a corner of his eye he saw that the mining engineer had also gotten out of the coach. The engineer was

44

unarmed but he looked sympathetic. "I don't figure to let a lame horse pull a stage six miles uphill."

"We'll do the figurin'," Gil snapped. "You do the drivin'. Climb back on that box and let's go."

They were crowding Wes. He couldn't back another step without pushing them aside. Surprise was his only chance. As Wes swung to face them his left fist drove to Fred Dillon's chin and his right drew a forty-five.

Fred went flat on his back. Gil felt something punch at his ribs and knew it was the bore of a gun.

"Blast him, Fred!" Frustrated fury made splotches on Gil's face. With a gun at his ribs he couldn't draw himself. But Fred lay in the clear, ten feet away.

Wes couldn't watch them both. He didn't see Fred come out of his shock and draw a gun. He heard the roar as a wild bullet whipped through fir boughs by the trail. Then the engineer's voice. "There's a law against shooting stage drivers." He'd kicked Fred Dillon's wrist and sent the gun spinning.

A breath later Wes disarmed Gil. "Thanks." He looked gratefully at the engineer. "If you'll hand me that ball of twine in the tool box I'll pig-string these smarties."

The Dillons were made to lie face down while Wes tied them ankle and wrist. "You're not passengers any more. You're freight. And I'm throwing you off at Hodge's."

Turning back to the Halfway House for a fresh horse made them two hours late. Wes didn't release the Dillons till he was ready to pull out. He gave them back their guns but kept all cartridges. "You can either walk," he told them, "or wait for tomorrow's stage."

Fred gave him a sullen stare.

Gil smiled but the smile was deadly. "We'll look you up," he promised, "when we get to Aspen."

Wes cracked his whip and the stage moved out. The engineer now shared the outside seat with him, letting the woman have the coach to herself. "That was a threat. A threat to gun you on sight. I'm Harv Random, if you need a witness."

Wes shrugged. "Threats are cheap. Got the makings?"

Random brought out makings and they rolled cigarets.

Half an hour later they were creeping along a ledge with a sheer precipice yawning close to the off wheels. It was Random's first trip up here and he held his breath.

Wes looked at him and grinned. "It's not so bad in summertime. Kinda scary, though, in winter. In the winter we take off the wheels and put on runners. The freighters do the same thing. Last winter Jeff Conly came along here with a load of eggs. His rear runners went over the edge and Jeff jumped. Didn't hurt him any. But his mules and his eggs fell two thousand feet straight down."

They kept climbing, twisting torturously to timber line and then on up along bare rock ledges.

At the pass Random relaxed and Wes rested the horses briefly. Presently they wheeled on to the highest gold camp on the divide. The Post Office department

46

called it Sparkhill but the miners called it Independence. Fresh horses and two passengers were waiting there.

While the change was being made, Wes crossed to Langstaff's store. A man stood by a black saddle horse at the rack. "Been waitin' for you, driver. My name's Fink."

Wes looked at the black horse. "That's the one," he decided. "Who picked him up?"

"A posse from Aspen. They're still out lookin' for my rifle and clothes."

"The guy dropped 'em down some shaft," Wes guessed. "Did he leave any sign at your cabin? Anything that'd give us a line on him?"

Fink shook his head. "Nope. He just went in and helped himself. Rode away on a shod horse leadin' mine. Used mine to hold up the stage with, then turned him loose."

Wes went over to the Grand Hotel, a three storey frame built five years ago in the camp's heydey. This was the regular eating stop and he joined Harv Random at a table. Others were local miners.

"What about this new strike down at Aspen?" one of them asked Wes. "They say a low-grade claim called the *Lost Friend* went into bonanza overnight."

"Must've happened since I left town," Wes said.

Random showed an alert interest. "I'm on my way for a look at it," he told them, "representing minority stockholders at Leadville. Three-fifths of the stock, I understand, is held by an Aspen man named Bayard."

Wes gulped his food and stood up. "Let's go. We're two hours late."

He went out and found Fink waiting at the stage. "One thing's been puzzlin' me," Fink confided. "About what that holdup man grabbed outa my cabin."

"Yeh?" Wes prompted.

"I had two rifles in there. They stood side by side in a corner. Ammunition for both was on the table. One was an old-fashioned rimfire .44 — an 1866 model. The other was an 1885 model Hotchkiss repeater."

"So what?"

"He took the rimfire and left the up-to-date model right there. Don't hardly seem natural."

Wes chewed it over in his mind. "No, it doesn't seem natural," he agreed. "If I needed a rifle to hold up a stage with, I'd grab the best one in sight."

His passengers got into the coach and Wes drove on. From here the grade was down and he made brisk time. His mind fastened on the oddity mentioned by Fink. Why would the bandit choose the less accurate of two rifles?

Presently he passed the scene of the holdup. Hoofmarks of the posse were there but the spot was now deserted. Wes drove thoughtfully on. He was trotting into the last change station, Deane's Camp, when the answer jolted him.

The bandit's only reason for raiding the shack had been to equip himself with a disguise. Clothes other than his own; a rifle other than his own; a horse other than his own.

If his own rifle was a Hotchkiss 45–70, he'd shy away from taking Fink's. Instead he'd take the rimfire .44, quite distinct in length and shape from his own. The range would be point blank, so accuracy wasn't important; at least it was less important than disguise.

A fact popped into Wes Brian's head and he confirmed it while a hostler was hooking up six fresh horses. "You were in that rifle shoot down at Aspen on the Fourth of July, weren't you, Pete?"

Pete grinned ruefully. "Didn't do me any good, though. Jim Downing won it, hands down."

"Myron Lockwood took second place, didn't he, using a Springfield army rifle?"

The hostler scratched his head, thinking back. "Lockwood took second place," he remembered. "But not with a Springfield. He had a brand new Hotchkiss 45–70."

As he drove on, a sense of complete conviction filled Wes. Lockwood was the man, all right. He'd shied off from using a rifle like his own; and he had a whip-cut ear.

Yet the whip-cut couldn't be proved. Lockwood claimed it was a thorn scratch and who could say it wasn't? Nor would the make of a rifle carry weight in court. *I know it's Lockwood but I can't prove it; and I'd better keep my mouth shut till I can.*

It was well after dark when Wes clattered across a bridge at the east end of Cooper Avenue. From there on saloons lined the road on either side. The woman in the coach called to him. "Let me off at Hunter Street, please."

Wes pulled up at Frank Olive's Corner Saloon and the woman got out. Two women from the Row were waiting to meet her and the three headed south toward Durant.

Wes drove on past Charley Boyd's *Comique*. Off-shift muckers filled the walks, dusty, shaggy figures in the glow of street lamps. His other passengers would put up at the Clarendon, so Wes kept on to Mill Street.

Traffic there stopped him a moment. It was curtain time at the Rink Opera House, a block farther on. Many were heading that way. An open carriage rolled north along Mill and turned left at this corner. In it Wes saw two theatre-bound couples. Two young and pretty girls each with a handsome escort.

One of the men was Myron Lockwood. The Swiss Bell Ringers were billed at the Rink and it wasn't strange that Lockwood should be taking Phyllis Wilbur there. He'd been rushing her for weeks and the whole town knew it. A sense of frustration bit Wes. What the whole town didn't know, and would never believe, was that Lockwood had held up a stage.

The other girl had red hair and Wes saw that she was Honora Norman. He wasn't surprised to find her already popular in Aspen. Beautiful young girls didn't grow on trees, hereabouts. Frank Bayard, who was squiring her tonight, must have dated her almost at sight. Wes saw the carriage pull up at Monarch Street, in front of the brilliantly lighted Rink.

He turned his stage south on Mill and at the next corner let his passengers out at the Clarendon. After delivering the mail and express pouches he drove on to the Carson barn.

A barn man handed him a letter. "It just came in on the Ashcroft stage, Wes."

The postmark was Ashcroft, a mining settlement thirteen miles up Castle Creek. The letter, on stationery of the Covert House at Ashcroft, was addressed to W. Brian in care of the Carson stage line at Aspen.

When he opened it the signature puzzled him. He didn't know anyone named Hostetter.

Mr. W. Brian,
Aspen,
Dear sir:

The roof of the east stope is a little soft. It ought to be shored up.

J. Hostetter.

"The east stope of what?" Wes wondered aloud. "And who does he think I am, anyway?"

CHAPTER
SIX

On his off day Wes slept till nearly noon. A thirty-mule jack train was filing by as he went out to eat. Ore for the Leadville smelters. The Aspen smelter, badly designed and never a success, was shut down just now. Ore was being stacked high on vacant lots all over town. It came down from the mines faster than it could be freighted out over the passes. The demand for mules and wagons far exceeded the supply.

But it wouldn't be for long. Two railroads were racing this way and soon there'd be no need to freight by cart and hoof. November at the latest would see locomotives steaming into Aspen. And on that day the Carson stage line would shut down forever.

Wes bought today's Aspen *Times* and went into the Delmonico for a noon breakfast. Waiting for his order he read the headlines.

TURN THE BOOM LOOSE AND LET 'ER RIP!

This whole issue was in that vein. Editor Clark Wheeler was at his exuberant best today. The D & R G, he announced, had laid forty miles of narrow gauge track in the last three weeks. Its head engineer,

McMurtrie, was a wizard. But at that, Wheeler prophesied, the standard gauge Midland would beat its rival to Aspen.

A waitress noticed the headlines. "Which one are you betting on?" she asked.

"I got ten bucks on the Midland," Wes grinned. "But I lose my job either way it goes."

Since neither road was coming via Independence Pass, there were no construction camps along the stage route. Both lines had tunneled the divide well to the north and were using canyon routes to hit Roaring Fork considerably below Aspen. From there they'd lay track upstream, approaching this boom silver town from the west.

A drummer had been slugged and robbed last night on Hyman Street. Wheeler used it as a springboard for an editorial. Aspen was overrun, he complained, with thugs and brace game gamblers. "McEvoy should give them just twenty-four hours to leave town."

Which reminded Wes that he had a message for McEvoy from the Leadville sheriff. About keeping an eye on the Dillon brothers. But no hurry about it, Wes thought as he went out. He'd left those bullies stranded at Mountain Boy Park and they couldn't get here till nightfall, when the next stage came in.

Saloon trade was already brisk, although the faro banks wouldn't open till midafternoon. The *Comique* was advertising SAVED FROM THE GALLOWS for tonight; and Colonel Willard — according to the *Times* he was related to the hotel Willards of Washington —

was exercising the new blooded carriage horses with which he'd just stocked his livery stable.

A display of suits in Julius Berg's window reminded Wes that his own was getting shabby. It would have to do until pay day, for he'd left nearly all his cash with Frank Bayard.

Thought of Bayard reminded him of last night, with Bayard taking Honora Norman to the Rink. Time he was looking her up himself, Wes decided. She hadn't been far from his mind since she'd boarded his stage at Leadville, four mornings ago.

He walked briskly to the Clarendon.

"Is Miss Norman in?"

The desk clerk nodded toward the dining room. "She's in there with her father."

Wes looked curiously at the registry book. She hadn't mentioned a father. The Monday registrations showed she'd been given room 30. But the Tuesday page showed she'd been joined by a Roger Norman and that the two were now sharing suite 22–24.

Wes looked into the dining room. She was at a table with a thin, white-haired gentleman whose pink-veined face had a scrubbed look, like he'd just come from a barber. Wes couldn't remember having seen him before, yet the man's scarred face seemed oddly familiar.

He hung his hat and gunbelt on a lobby rack. Entering the dining room Wes advanced eagerly to Honora's table. "Hello there, Miss Norman. Hope you haven't run into any more holdup men. Saw you pass by last night, on your way to . . ."

54

"If you're here to apologize," she broke in coldly, "you're too late. A fine preacher's son you are! Please go away and don't ever speak to me again!"

Clearly she meant it. Her tone was scathing and contempt snapped from her eyes. The man opposite her seemed more self-conscious than hostile. He leaned forward with a murmur of caution. "I wouldn't make an issue of it, Honora . . ."

"What the heck's goin' on?" Wes exploded. "You aren't mistakin' me for a patch of poison ivy, are you? What have I done?"

"Pretend you don't know!" The retort was bitter. "Play innocent! It was the most despicable thing I ever heard of! I've far more respect for that stage robber than I have for you. If I had my way you'd go to prison for it. Now get out of my sight and stay out!"

The girl's voice rose to the edge of hysteria and tears welled in her eyes.

Wes gaped for a moment, astonished and confused. Then, with his face burning, he turned and walked out. Any further word of his would only add fuel to her fury.

He slammed on his hat and buckled on his gunbelt. As he left the hotel he bumped into a man coming in. The man had a carnation in his buttonhole. An eagerness about him might mean he was on his way to follow up last night's date.

"Well, well! If it's not my client the stage driver!" Bayard gave Wes a patronizing clap on the shoulder. "By the way, I haven't invested that money of yours yet. I'm still looking for a good buy."

"Take your time," Wes said absently. He brushed by and turned down the Durant Street walk. He was in no mood to talk about mining stock. Only one thing mattered now. Why was the girl sore at him? What did she think he'd done?

After a dozen steps a thought stopped him. Only one man in town hated Wes. Myron Lockwood. Lockwood hated him for guessing the guilt in the holdup. Last night the man had been one in a foursome with Honora Norman. He wasn't her date, but he'd been in her company all evening.

To get even, he might have poisoned the girl's mind against Wes Brian. Nothing else made sense.

The thought spun Wes around and hurried him back into the Clarendon. He rushed up to Lockwood's room and knocked. There was no answer. He opened the unlocked door and found the room empty.

Nor was Lockwood in the hotel's barroom. Passing the dining room Wes glanced in and saw Frank Bayard. The big yellow-haired broker had drawn up a chair to the Norman table and was making himself at home.

To Wes all that mattered now was finding Lockwood. *I'll twist his neck, till he owns up just what he told her!* A fierce fever to do just that sent him storming down to Cooper Avenue.

As far as he knew, Lockwood lived by his wits. The man had no business or office. In early afternoon he'd likely be found in one of the three fancy saloons: the Abbey, the Branch, or the Brick.

56

Wes looked first in the Abbey, then in the Branch. Lockwood was in neither. He tried the Brick. "Seen Myron Lockwood?"

"Not today," the bartender said. "But he generally stops in about this time, for a quickie."

Waiting here would be smarter than hunting him through the town. Wes took a beer to a table. Trade was still slack, this early. The faro man was getting his layout ready. Two cowhands from Woody Creek were trading treats at the bar.

At a rear table three Tourtelotte Park miners were talking shop. "Johnny had plenty of hard luck in his day," one said, "but this takes the biscuit! Sellin' out for a song like that, just before his claim made the headlines!"

"Where did he go?"

"Headed fer Telluride, I heard, by way of Ashcroft and Gunnison."

The third man shook his head sadly. "Poor old Johnny Hostetter! Luck sure played him a dirty trick!"

Hostetter! The name aroused an echo in Wes Brian's mind. A letter had come to him from Ashcroft. A mystery letter signed J. Hostetter.

Must've got me mixed with someone else.

Wes was too absorbed with another mystery to keep his mind long on this one. The mystery of a girl's resentment. The key to it was sure to be Lockwood. Worse than a stage robber! she'd said. Had Lockwood hinted that Wes, the driver, was in cahoots with the bandit? That driver and bandit had met later to split the loot? That very trick had been put over once, on the stage line to St. Elmo. Wes fixed his eyes impatiently on the doorway, waiting for Lockwood to come in.

In a little while Lockwood *did* come in. "The same, Joe," he said, and took a stand at the top of the bar. Joe slid him a straight Bourbon. Lockwood held it to the light, for the moment not seeing Brian.

He wore no gun. His hat today was low-crowned, with a chin-strap and with a wide brim curled upward on the sides. That and dark sideburns growing down his temples made him look like a dashing young *hidalgo*.

Wes wasted no time. He moved to the bar and stood at Lockwood's elbow. "Just what did you tell her?" he demanded, keeping his voice low.

His sudden appearance startled Lockwood. "This another riddle?" he asked cagily. At their last meeting he'd been tricked into looking at a mirror.

"You were out with a lady last night. Just what slimy lie did you tell on me?" Wes didn't raise his voice and six other men in the room hadn't yet sensed a quarrel. Joe was polishing glassware and didn't look this way.

Lockwood forced a smile and answered quietly. "Your name didn't come up. It wasn't important enough. Why would I want to lie about you?"

"Because I'm the only one you didn't fool with a mask. You've got ten seconds by the barroom clock. Talk or fight."

Wes drew his gun and broke it at the hinge, shaking the shells out into his hand. He put the empty gun back in its holster and glanced down the bar. Others in the room hadn't looked this way. Two cowboys were tossing

58

for the drinks and three hard rock men were still discussing Hostetter.

Nine of the ten seconds ticked by before Lockwood spoke. "Why don't you ask McEvoy? Or Sheriff Hooper? Or Wheeler of the *Times?* Or Lawyer Downing? Any of them can tell you why she'd like to have you staked out on an ant hill, smeared head to foot with molasses."

Lockwood's thin, confident smile warned Wes that he'd better hold his punch. Maybe he'd gone off half-cocked. "McEvoy?" he questioned confusedly. "What does *he* know about it?"

"Go ask him." Myron Lockwood turned his back on Wes and raised his voice. "Another of the same, Joe."

The scratch on his ear was healed now. Brawling with the man here, or accusing him without proof, would only make Wes ridiculous. "I'll see McEvoy," he said. "If it's not like you say, I'll be right back."

Wes went out and hurried to the city jail. Marshal John McEvoy, a solid, capable officer with clear gray eyes and a brown mustache, looked up from his desk. A teasing smile formed on his round, sunburned face.

"Come to give yourself up, Brian?"

"For what?"

"A lady was in to swear out a warrant. She wanted to slap you in the Bastille for life. She even tried to hire a special prosecutor; but he talked her out of it."

So Lockwood had told the truth, after all! Dismay settled over Wes.

"Your name's mud with her," McEvoy chuckled. "You can't blame her much — after that nice, clean fun you boys had at the Abbey bar Monday night. A gal doesn't like to see her old man treated that way . . ."

"The Major!" Wes exclaimed. "He's her father? That old soak?"

"Why not? We all have our ups and downs. Too bad you have to take the rap for it, though. You're the only one she can prove was there. The Abbey barkeep clams up on it. Says he can't remember . . ."

"I just went along to make sure they didn't . . ." Wes broke off helplessly. He couldn't deny he was there. Somehow Honora Norman knew it and she'd never forgive him.

"She'll take him back east with her after the tenth," McEvoy explained. "He's needed as a witness in the Jenner case. I sure don't envy the girl — keeping the Major sober that long. Some night he'll feel a thirst and sneak out to the nearest bar."

"She left him alone last night," Wes remembered.

"Not alone," McEvoy corrected. "The McLaughlins are helping her ride herd on him. Last night they had old Professor Tweedy play chess with him till the show was over at the Rink. Turns out the Major used to be a chess champion."

Wes started out, then remembered a message from the sheriff at Leadville. He told McEvoy about the Dillon brothers. "But they won't be in till stage time tonight. I left them stranded in Mountain Boy Park."

"You're wrong," McEvoy said. "They didn't wait for the stage. They bummed a ride on a freighter and got here at noon. Officer Webb spotted them. They've got a record at Fair Play. And they used to run with Alf

Jenner. So I warned Sheriff Hooper and he's putting a special guard on at the county jail."

"In case they try to break Jenner out?"

"That's right. Meantime better keep out of their way, young fella. They're bad medicine."

"I won't go hunting for them," Wes promised.

He walked restlessly down Galena to Hyman. The Dillon brothers, Myron Lockwood, the mystery note from Ashcroft — all were brushed from his mind as he thought about Honora Norman. How could he square himself? How could he convince her?

She'd refuse to see him if he called at the Clarendon. At dawn tomorrow he must drive east with his stage and wouldn't be back for three days. He couldn't bear to have her despise him for that long.

Maybe she'd read a note if he sent it by messenger. He'd tell her the simple truth. Maybe she'd believe him and maybe she'd wouldn't. But it was worth a try.

In the same note he could warn her about Gil and Fred Dillon. Those plugs weren't over here for their health. Maybe they planned to break Jenner out of jail. But it would be smarter and easier if they merely got rid of a witness. The state's star witness against Jenner was Roger Norman. Honora should be warned about it. She should ask the sheriff to furnish a bodyguard for her father till trial day.

Wes hurried to his rooming house on East Hyman. The place had shops downstairs and a double row of cheap rooms above. Narrow, dusty steps led to them. It was a shabby place, but a stage driver could hardly afford the Clarendon.

He must write that note and get it off right away. Wes opened the door of his room and went in. There was an iron bed, a table, a washstand, a chair and a curtained closet. He tossed his hat on the bed, sat down and reached for a pen.

He heard the step back of him — too late. A gun crashed on his head. As Wes slithered to the floor a second man came from the closet and kicked him in the face.

He lay on his back with Gil Dillon kneeling astride of him and pounding his chin and mouth and eyes. Blood gushed from a cut where the spurred boot of Fred Dillon raked him. "We'll learn him who to get fresh with," Gil grunted.

Fred kicked him again and again. And Gil kept pounding. Long after Wes lost consciousness they kept kicking and pounding.

"We'll learn him who to fool with, Fred." Gil raised the stage driver's head and bumped it hard on the floor.

"Be a long time before he skins another stage team, Gil." Fred gave a final kick and the two men backed from the room.

No one had seen them come in. No one saw them leave.

CHAPTER
SEVEN

TURN THE BOOM LOOSE AND LET 'ER RIP! It was a standard banner line in the *Times* during those final days of August, the year 1887. It wouldn't be long now! The railroads were coming fast, smashing tracklaying records with nearly every shift. The Midland made construction history as it blasted its Hagerman tunnel through the divide and came streaking down the Frying Pan — only to be matched by the D & R G with its equally prodigious spurt through Eagle River Canyon. Both would soon come racing up Roaring Fork to Aspen, the Midland on the south bank and the Little Giant on the north.

"It's a horse race!" chuckled Joe, the Brick Saloon bartender. "But my money goes on the Midland."

"Put mine on the Rio Grande," echoed his customer of the moment, Myron Lockwood. So another bet was posted. Hundreds of them, ranging from a dollar to a thousand, were posted at bars all over Aspen.

"They'll both be here by November," gloated a hoist man from Smuggler Mountain. "After that you can shoot my mule. Look what it says here." He read aloud an item from the *Times*.

The Midland has just received some handsome saloon cars with white oak and fine carvings, the smoking room enclosed with plate glass. These cars will be attached to all trains between Denver and Aspen without extra charge to passengers.

"You can shoot my mule too," a Tourtelotte Park man chimed in. "And throw away my snow shoes. Last trip I made over the range I went afoot, hip deep in drifts. Not even the stages could get through. Next time I'll be in a parlor car, ringin' fer the porter to come shine my boots."

The talk echoed all through Aspen. They'd join the GREAT OUTSIDE, when the tracks came. No more stage coaches; no more jack trains; no longer would a grim stone curtain wall them from the world.

With it all came reports of new and bigger strikes on Aspen Mountain. Ore wagons rumbled day and night into the town, stacking ore along the railroad right-of-ways. New brick buildings went up along Galena and Hyman. Saloons and faro games ran double shift. Investors flocked in by stage and saddle.

No wonder the *Times* gave less than a column to a mere assault case. Brawls were routine in Aspen these days and the affair at a Hyman Street rooming house was only another one.

Honora read about it in her room at the Clarendon.

Wesley Brian found unconscious in his room, bloody and brutally beaten! It made her vaguely uncomfortable.

She wished now she hadn't scolded him so bitterly. Not that he didn't deserve it. But after all it had done no good. And of course she'd never see him again.

What would they do with him? The town had no real hospital yet. It had grown too fast. What did they do with homeless young men when they were picked up horribly beaten?

Voices in the next room reminded her that her father and Tweedy were at it again. She went in there and stood behind Roger Norman's chair. It was six days since she'd brought him here. She felt sure his rehabilitation was well under way. Yesterday he hadn't even begged her for a drink.

So far the professor had won every game. Honora wanted it that way. It made a challenge for Roger Norman, a battle to be lost or won. And after all he was an old soldier.

"I'll beat him yet," he vowed, smiling up at his daughter. His wavy white hair was freshly cut and a clean shave made the sabre scar stand starkly on his cheek.

Honora leaned over and kissed him. "Of course you will, Dad."

A knock summoned her to the door. A bellboy was there. "Gentleman in the lobby to see you, Miss Norman."

She glanced toward Professor Tweedy and he nodded. The nod was a promise not to leave Roger Norman alone. The McLaughlins and Doctor Perry were helping her too. They all understood her problem.

A mere tinkle of glassware from the bar would be enough to tempt her father.

The caller, she supposed, was Frank Bayard. He'd been persistently attentive and she liked him. Twice he'd taken her out. And yesterday he'd sold her interest in the *Little Lucy* at a figure slightly more than she'd hoped for.

But when she got down to the lobby the waiting man was a stranger. He was in leathers and puttees and had a pleasant, tanned face.

"Miss Norman? I'm Harv Random of Leadville."

She placed him at once. Frank Bayard had told her about Random. He was a mining expert sent by minority stockholders of the *Lost Friend*. Bayard had been favorably impressed by him and as majority owner had appointed Random production manager of the mine. The new bonanza was now entirely in the engineer's hands. Already he had full crews at work there.

"Won't you sit down, Mr. Random?"

They found seats on the lobby divan. "I just called on a friend and he gave me a message for you. He's Wesley Brian, the stage driver."

Surprise made her forget, for the moment, her resentment against Brian. "I read about him. Is he badly hurt?"

Random nodded. "He thinks the men who hurt him came here for one of two reasons: to break a killer named Jenner out of jail; or to eliminate the only witness who can convict Jenner."

With a shock Honora realized he meant her father. At once she saw the logic of it. Until trial day a constant threat would hang over Roger Norman.

"Wesley Brian sent you to warn me?"

"To warn both you and the sheriff. I've already spoken to the sheriff."

"And what did he say?"

"He said he'll assign a bodyguard to protect Major Norman from now till September tenth. A deputy named Hearn. Hearn will take a room across from your father's; at meals he'll be at a nearby table."

Honora was both grateful and relieved. "But why," she wondered, "didn't someone else think of this?"

Harv Random looked at her with a wise smile. "Perhaps because Wes Brian's put in more time thinking about you than anyone else has. Also he knows better than anyone else just how mean those Dillons are." He told her about the Mountain Boy Park scuffle. "Last thing Gil Dillon said to him was: 'We'll look you up when we get to town.' They looked him up and beat him up before they'd been here three hours."

"Why," Honora demanded, "doesn't the sheriff put them in jail?"

"The police questioned them," Random explained, "but they've got an airtight alibi. A man swears he was playing stud with them when it happened. Wes didn't see them. He was hit from behind. Which leaves no case against Gil and Fred Dillon."

"Where is he now? I mean Wesley Brian."

"At what passes for a hospital in Doctor Ed Coxon's back yard on West Hopkins. It's just an old bunkshack, with a Mexican acting as combination cook and nurse. The stage people are footing the bill. They're grateful to Wes for defending a lame stage horse; and they figure that's what got him beat up by the Dillons."

"How badly is he hurt?"

"They bunged him up enough to kill most men. But that boy's tough. He's coming out of it fast."

A bland voice broke in. "What's this? My mine manager making love to my best girl?"

Frank Bayard had come in unnoticed.

Honora looked up at the broker's handsome, ruddy face. "He brought me a message from the stage driver. About those terrible Dillons."

Random got to his feet. "I better be getting back to the mine now. Want to start shoring up that stope. Which reminds me. Kind of odd the way I heard about it, Bayard. Maybe you can explain it. I can't. Take a look."

He brought out a letter and let them see it. One look and the laugh died on Frank Bayard's face.

It was dated at Ashcroft last Tuesday and addressed to W. Brian at Aspen. It warned of a soft roof of a stope. The signature was J. Hostetter.

"Brian gave it to me just now," Random puzzled. "Asked me if I could figure it out. Says he doesn't know anyone named Hostetter. I told him a man of that name used to own the *Lost Friend* mine."

"But that's *your* mine, isn't it, Mr. Bayard?" The question came curiously from Honora Norman. "Why would he write Wesley Brian about it?"

Bayard fanned himself with his hat. To hide his confusion he brought out a handkerchief and mopped his face. He was in a corner and had to think fast.

"Yes, why would he?" echoed Harv Random, no less puzzled than the girl. "Since the mine's yours, why didn't he write to *you?*"

Frank Bayard tried to shrug it away. "I'll ask Johnny Hostetter next time I write him. There's no doubt some simple explanation. By the way, Honora, here's something the Major might like to read." The book he brought from his pocket was Creasy's "Fifteen Decisive Battles of History."

"Thank you. I'm sure he will." Honora accepted the book, smiling at Random as he took his leave.

In a few more minutes Bayard himself was gone. He'd brought the book merely as an excuse to spend the rest of the afternoon with Honora. But now the bombshell of Hostetter's letter sent him hurrying back to his office.

Again he locked himself in, drew the blinds and opened the safe. He took out the certificate which Hostetter had assigned to Wesley Brian. Patient hours with an ink erasure had accomplished the substitution of his own name. The assignee was now Frank Bayard. Only a microscope could detect any tampering. Eleven letters in each name was pure luck, leaving only a shadowy "y" between the "k" and the "B."

There'd be no occasion for any suspicious scrutiny — unless someone made a charge of fraud. A million dollars was at stake. Later assays all showed about eight hundred ounces of silver to the ton. The risk was that

Hostetter might return to Aspen; or write to someone here; or that some sharp mind like Harv Random's might put two and two together. Since Hostetter had transferred the mine to Bayard, why should he write about it to a stage driver?

Here in this safe was an envelope holding three hundred dollars. On it was written, "To be invested for Wesley Brian."

For the sake of appearances Bayard decided he'd better invest it at once. In what?

His eye fell on another envelope and he took it thoughtfully from the safe.

Here was a deed to an improved quarter-section forty miles down Roaring Fork, where a stream called Cattle Creek came in. Bayard had acquired it by foreclosing a loan. The place was good only for livestock and was a long way out of the mining belt. As a mining broker Frank Bayard had no use for it.

But for a young man interested in horses and cattle, it would be a bargain at two thousand dollars. The improvements alone, cabin, shed, fence and well, were worth that.

An idea inspired Bayard. When it jelled he put the title in his pocket, locked the office and walked to Doctor Ed Coxon's place on West Hopkins.

A plank shed along the alley back of Coxon's cottage had six rooms in a line. In one of them Wesley Brian lay on a cot, his face patched and his head bandaged. Bayard found him reading today's *Times*.

"Hello, Client. Looks like they kinda worked you over."

Wes grinned ruefully. "They used everything but dynamite." His friendly tone reassured Bayard. The Hostetter letter clearly hadn't aroused any suspicion.

"Just figured out a smart way to invest that three hundred dollars of yours. Look, Wes. You're no miner. You don't know beans about mining and you care less. But you're an expert with cows and horses. Right?"

"I know horses," Wes admitted. "What's the deal?"

Bayard tossed him the deed to a quarter-section on Cattle Creek. "It's a giveaway at two thousand, and I'd accept three hundred for a down payment. Take your note for the balance at five percent, and give you as much time as you want. There's a good three-room cabin, shed, well, fence — and a million acres of free government grass right there handy."

A glow in Brian's eyes encouraged Bayard. He went on with details calculated to make a stock lover's pulse quicken. "A great cow country down there, fella. Your trading point'd be Glenwood Springs and I know a banker there. I can give you a letter to him and he'll likely stock the place for you, for chattel paper." All the while Bayard was thinking: *It's forty miles down the valley. In a cattle country where people don't even talk about mines. Once he settles there, Aspen drops out of his life forever.*

"It sure sounds good." Wes Brian's voice was wistful. He'd always wanted a place of his own.

"Comes just at the right time for you, too. Your stage job'll be washed up, when the railroads get here. You'll have to make another start and where could you find a sweeter one than this?"

"Where could I?" Wes admitted. Then a stubborn look came to his face as he handed the title back to Bayard. "I'll take you up on it," he said, "just as soon as I tend to a couple of things here in Aspen."

"What things? Maybe I can help you."

"First I want to square myself with the Normans." Wes added a bit sheepishly, "They think I was in on that horse play at the cemetery."

"Sure." Bayard gave a sympathetic nod. "The Normans are friends of mine and I'll put in a good word for you. So consider yourself squared. What else you got on your mind?"

"A man held up my stage. And I'm not going to let him get away with it. I don't aim to leave Aspen till he's nailed for it."

Bayard cocked an eyebrow. "You got any idea who he is?"

"I *know* who he is. I whip-lashed his left ear. And he used a .44 rimfire rifle because his own's a 45–70 Hotchkiss."

The eye under the cocked brow narrowed. "Want to put a name to him?"

"Not yet," Wes said. "He's a man who needed quick cash so he stuck up a stage for it. Soon as I nail him, bring around that Cattle Creek deal and we'll do business."

It was all Bayard could get out of him. He left the place and walked east along Hopkins. Who, he wondered, had Brian pegged for the stage robber?

At Mill Street he glanced to the left and saw a carriage drawn up a block north. In it were Phyllis

72

Wilbur and Myron Lockwood. The girl's father, Joshua B. Wilbur, was pacing about in a vacant lot at the northwest corner of Mill and Main. The New Yorker was promoting many projects in this silver town, among them an opera house and a fancy hotel. The lot he was looking at now had been mentioned as a site for the hotel.

The couple in the carriage brought a faint smile to Bayard. He wondered why the Wilburs couldn't see through Lockwood. Lockwood called himself a speculator, but really he was just a fortune hunting gambler. The stake he was playing for was the Wilbur fortune; and by the way he was making time with Phyllis, it wouldn't take him long to get it.

Halfway across Mill Street a thought stopped Bayard. He remembered a scene last Tuesday noon, at the Clarendon hitchrack. Lockwood buying back a poker check; and some glib remark about wanting to keep a four-figure balance in the First National of Leadville.

At the time it had mildly puzzled Bayard. He happened to know that Lockwood was in arrears with his room rent at the Clarendon. So it wasn't likely that the man had a tidy bank balance, at Leadville or anywhere else.

A whip-cut on his left ear? Yes, Bayard recalled seeing a scratch there early last week. Right after Lockwood's horseback trip to Leadville. And Lockwood owned a Hotchkiss rifle!

When pertinent details came back to Bayard one by one, they made a pattern. Myron Lockwood!

Conviction flashed through Bayard. He was sure of it now, as sure of it as was Brian himself. Lockwood had robbed a stage for cash with which to pick up a worthless check.

The check would have washed up his prospects with Phyllis Wilbur. Bayard looked again at the carriage a block north. A sense of power came to him. He could make Lockwood dance, if he wanted to.

Frank Bayard wheeled and walked resolutely to the next corner north. He stopped by the carriage, tipping his hat to Phyllis. "See you a minute, Myron? Small matter of business. You'll excuse us, won't you, Phyllis?"

Lockwood looked slightly annoyed. But he got out and followed Bayard a few steps up the walk.

Out of hearing Bayard said bluntly: "Just thought I'd warn you, Myron. About that stage driver. Soon as he's out of bed he figures to queer you with the Wilburs."

Lockwood was plainly startled. But he kept his voice low. "Queer me? How?"

"I just left him, Myron. He's got a crazy idea it was you who held up his stage. Said something about a whip-cut on your ear. Said you passed up a new model rifle to use an old rimfire. Said you used the loot to buy back a bum check. Said he checked at that bank on his next trip to Leadville and you never did have even a three-figure balance there."

"He's lying!" Lockwood's face had strain on it but his voice was still low and guardedly even. "It's a cock and bull story he cooked up out of thin air."

74

"Sure it is, Myron. He didn't fool *me* with it, not for a minute. Just the same he'll unload it on old man Wilbur. A cagey customer, Wilbur. When he gets the wind up, he shies off like a buggy horse. Like he shied away from that merger up in the Park. He never takes a chance — especially with that girl of his. One breath of scandal and he'll yank Phyllis back to New York."

Joshua Wilbur was moving toward them and Bayard waved a hand. "Hello there, Mr. Wilbur. Bar silver went up to a dollar six cents this morning. Did you hear? Be seeing you, Myron. Keep him guessing, Phyllis." The broker walked jauntily up Mill to Hyman, stopping in at the first bar.

"Rye highball, please."

As he held it to the light, Frank Bayard's plump blond face smiled back at him from the bar mirror. "Here's to murder!" he grinned; and the bartender thought it was a joke.

It wasn't, though, and no one knew it better than Bayard. He'd watched Lockwood's eyes and seen murder there. One bullet in the dark, in Doc Coxon's back yard tonight, and Lockwood need no longer fear Wes Brian.

Bayard sipped his liquor, preening his own smartness in setting up the target. He need lift no hand himself. He'd be up at the Clarendon, dating Honora Norman, while Lockwood did the dirty work on Brian. There'd be no need now to lure Brian to a Cattle Creek ranch.

Leave it to Lockwood. From here on he'd be a cat's-paw for Bayard. *He'll do as I say! I can make him dance — or kill!"*

It was perfect — foolproof even for Lockwood. For when they found Brian dead in that alley cabin, whom would they suspect? Not Lockwood, nor Frank Bayard, but Gil and Fred Dillon.

CHAPTER
EIGHT

As twilight faded, Wes sat propped up on the cot in room number four, at Coxon's, waiting for Alfredo to take away his supper tray. There were six rooms, all fronting a leaf-strewn back yard. A moan came from number three, whose occupant was a cave-in casualty. Wes looked out the open door at the moonlit yard, darkened on one side by the shadow of a cottonwood. A cart creaked along an alley back of this long plank shed. A woman took her leave from number six, where she'd been visiting her sick husband. After her steps died away Wes heard only the gurgle of a ditch running down the Hopkins Street gutter.

It was too early for sleep. Restless, Wes lighted an oil lamp by the cot. He picked up the *Times* again. Colorow and his Utes, the paper said, were on the rampage near Rangeley. The Aspen militia had been ordered out to fight them. Governor Alva Adams himself was taking command, with headquarters at Glenwood Springs.

Alfredo came in for the supper tray. "You should be asleep, señor," he reproved gently. "Shall I blow the lamp?"

"Not yet, Alfredo. And stop babyin' me. I may look sick, all swathed up like this, but I'm feelin' fine. Tomorrow I'm moving out."

The attendant shook his head. "Not so soon, I think."

"You'll need the space," Wes argued, "now that you've put someone in number two." Room two, directly east of Wes Brian's, had been the only one vacant.

"But you are wrong, señor. Number two she is still empty."

"That's funny. Thought I heard someone moving around in there, little while ago."

"I will go and see." Alfredo went out and was gone less than a minute. "She is empty, señor. But you are right. Someone was there. When I clean this morning I have shut the door but now she is open. Perhaps it is a tramp who looks for a place to sleep."

The Mexican took the tray and went out. Wes Brian rolled a smoke thoughtfully. If a tramp had sneaked into the next room to steal a night's sleep, why wasn't he still there?

Who else would prowl this row of back yard rooms? And why?

The Dillon brothers, Wes remembered only too well, had sneaked into his Hyman Street room to beat him up. Would they try it again? Not likely. Beating him up once should satisfy them.

His only other known enemy was Myron Lockwood. *He knows I'm on to him. And he'd sure like to burn me down.*

78

A man bold enough to hold up a stage would be bold enough to kill off a witness.

If Lockwood planned a job like that tonight, how would he go about it? *First he'd need to know what room I'm in.*

A prowl at nightfall would tell the man that much. Each of the six rooms had an alley window. Just before light faded, the man could slip along the alley and peer into each room. Finding one room vacant he might enter it by the alley window and wait his chance.

Alfredo had looked into number two but he hadn't looked under its cot. It was hard to imagine Myron Lockwood hiding under a cot. But some thug killer hired by Lockwood might do it. There were men in Aspen who'd cut a throat for fifty dollars.

Wes Brian's alley window had the blind drawn. No one could spy through it. What about number two's window?

The possibilities nagged Wes and made him get out of bed. His bare feet padded to a closet where they'd hung his clothes. He slipped on his socks and pants, leaving his boots there. His holster belt hung from a peg and he took the gun from it.

Then he stepped out into the moonlit yard and looked both ways along the shed. A thin moan came from number four. Five and six were dark; but the patient in number one had his lamp burning.

With his gun alert, Wes opened number two's door. Enough moonlight filtered in to show that the cot wasn't occupied. Wes went softly inside and opened the room's closet. It was empty. He kneeled and poked his gun under the cot. No prowler was hiding there.

But the shade was up at the alley window. At twilight anyone could have looked in. Nor was the window locked. A man could raise the sash, climb over the sill, stay long enough to scout the premises, then fade off down the alley.

Would he come back in the deep of night? His victim would be asleep by then. Lockwood? Brian shook his head. It was too thin. Nothing to build it on except a footstep he'd heard in here at twilight, and the fact that Lockwood would like to see him dead.

Wes struck a match and lighted the cotside lamp. The room was shabby, and arranged exactly like his own. By scouting it the prowler could note the position of the cot in relation to the door. He could stand just inside the door, listen, watch the yard, see Alfredo deliver the supper trays. He'd hear the several patients speak to Alfredo.

To watch and listen, he'd open the door a little and stand near it. Wes took the lamp there, stooped and looked for sign. Alfredo, a good *mozo*, had cleaned the room well. Yet a sliver of fresh mud was there; a cake the shape of a boot heel. A man jumping the Hopkins Street ditch could muddy his heel. A close look at the alley window showed another mud stain, where someone had climbed over the sill.

Wes put out the lamp and went back to his own room. His suspicions were solid, now. A man who sneaks in an alley window is certainly up to no good. Would he come back, after moonset?

If he comes he'll come to kill!

His cot had extra blankets at the foot and Wes made a roll of them. He laid the roll under the covers in the pose of a sleeper. Then he placed two pillows so that the top one had the shape and position of a sleeper's bandaged head. In bright moonlight the illusion would hardly fool anyone. In dim starlight it might. In two more hours the moon would sink behind the cottonwood on the west side of the yard.

Wes left the yard door ajar and blew out the lamp. The room's dimmest corner was the closet corner. Still in his sock feet, Wes put the only chair there and sat in it. He laid the gun on his knees and settled down to wait.

For Lockwood? For the Dillon brothers? For some hired thug picked up in one of the East Cooper dives? Or maybe for some harmless bum. Alfredo could be right. A tramp might sneak into number two to steal a night's sleep and then change his mind.

An hour went by with moonlight still lighting the yard. Beyond the yard a lamp in the doctor's cottage went out. Two warring cats yowled from the alley. But the shed itself was quiet; even number four seemed to be asleep. A crowd of teenagers romped along the Hopkins Street walk, homeward bound from a party.

The peace of night brought a sense of sheepishness to Wes. Here he was, sitting up with a gun, as suspicious and jumpy as an old maid. That attack on him at the rooming house had left him shying at shadows. A hundred to one Lockwood wouldn't come. Nor anyone else.

A carriage rolled along Hopkins, behind smart trotters, and a girl's laughter floated back from it. It might be the Wilbur girl, out for a moonlight spin with Lockwood. Or Honora Norman out with Bayard. The last thought shook Lockwood from Wes Brian's mind and made him concentrate on Honora. How well did she like Bayard? No question about how well he liked her. Frank Bayard was in dead earnest, all right. He'd do his best to persuade Honora to stay right here in Aspen.

And why shouldn't he? Bayard had looks and personality, and now that he controlled a bonanza he'd soon be a millionaire. He could build a mansion on Bullion Row for Honora and take her to Europe every year or so. Many of the silver kings lived that way. And once the railroads came, they could week-end in Denver at will.

The idea depressed Wes. He himself, while all that was going on, would be starting from scratch on a shoestring stock ranch down at Cattle Creek. He'd be completely out of Honora's orbit. If he ever saw her again it would be only a glimpse as she whizzed by in a private car. The new D & R G track was being laid via Glenwood Springs, not far from the quarter-section bargain Bayard was offering him.

The more he thought of it, the more of a bargain it seemed. Why, Wes wondered, was Bayard so anxious for him to take it? A small down payment and only five percent interest!

As he sat in the dark puzzling over it, a drowsiness came over Wes. His chin dropped. He sat up, shaking himself, and knew he'd dozed for perhaps half an hour. Moonlight no longer played in the yard. A black shadow from the cotton-wood covered all of it.

A dim gray rectangle marked the doorway. Except for that Wes could see only the outline of a cot. A pillow, which made a white lump at its head, told him where the cot was. A prowler in the doorway would see that much and nothing more.

But no prowler was coming. Wes was increasingly sure of it. He'd let imagination run away with reason. Mud on the sill of an alley window could have some simple explanation. Lots of things loomed like mysteries when they really weren't. Like that letter from Ashcroft about a stope. A mix-up of names, probably.

His friend Harv Random had the letter now. Maybe Harv could figure it out. Not that it made any great difference. What could a stage driver have to do with a mine stope?

Wes Brian's chin drooped, and again he dozed.

The roars of a gun awakened him. Thundering blasts shocked him like hammers pounding on his head.

A hatted silhouette stood in the doorway with flame spurting from its gun hand. Four stabs of flame and four booms — and four bullets through the whiteness of a pillow. Wes, in a dark corner, didn't move from his chair. It took the four shots to bring him completely awake. Then he picked up the forty-five from his lap and called out sharply, "Over this way, Mister."

Three more shots, then, two from the man in the doorway and one from Wes Brian. The man doubled forward, his hand still gripping an empty gun as his head and chest bumped the floor. Wes heard cries of alarm from the other patients. A rear window of the cottage went up and from it came the voice of Doctor Coxon. "What's going on out there? Get the police, Alfredo."

Wes went to the cotside stand and lighted the lamp. When he turned with it, the doorway framed two pale and staring faces. They were patients from rooms five and six. "Who is he?" one of them asked hoarsely.

"I'm not sure — yet," Wes said. The man lay face-down on the floor and didn't move. "We better not touch anything till the police get here."

"Is he dead?" number five asked.

"He looks dead to me," came huskily from number six. There was a stench of gunsmoke. Tiny pillow feathers were floating about the room. Number six, in his night shirt, came in for a closer look. "Great Jumpin' Bullfrogs! He sure stuffed that pillow full of lead! Good thing you wasn't sleepin' on it, brother!"

They heard running steps. Then one of McEvoy's men rushed in. He looked down at the man on the floor. "They tried it again, did they? Which one is he, Gil or Fred?"

"Look and see," Wes suggested.

The officer turned the dead man face up. "Gosh! It's Myron Lockwood! I can't believe it!"

"Smell his gun," Wes said. "Then count the bullets in my pillow."

CHAPTER
NINE

It was a long, tense evening for Frank Bayard. Needles of suspense pricked him as he waited at the Clarendon bar. The session of whist had lasted from suppertime till eleven; and under other circumstances, with Honora as his partner, he would have enjoyed every minute of it. But tonight was different. The pressure was on and Bayard could see it in Lockwood's face. Even Phyllis Wilbur had noticed it. "You're wool-gathering, Myron," she'd chided at her partner's third misplay.

When the girls left them, Bayard had invited Lockwood to the bar for a nightcap. "No thanks, Frank. I'm turning in." Calling for his key, Lockwood presumably had gone up to bed.

But Frank Bayard knew he hadn't. Watching from the barroom's north window he'd seen a tall silhouette slip away by the hotel's back door. The figure had angled across the hitching lot in a northwesterly direction. The Coxon cottage lay that way.

From then on Bayard had been careful to keep in the company of other men. He must stay right here till it was all over. Lockwood would use a gun, probably; but it might be a knife or a club.

Midnight struck and still no hue and cry was heard. Bayard kept constantly alert for a police whistle; or for some newsmonger rushing in to tell about murder at Coxon's.

Lockwood would need to wait till everything was quiet there. But there'd been time enough now. Why wasn't he back and in bed?

Maybe he was. A noiseless killing wouldn't be discovered till morning. An hour after midnight Bayard went up to Lockwood's room and knocked. When there was no response he knew the man wasn't there. Otherwise he'd be glad to show himself and so further the illusion that he'd never been out at all.

Bayard hurried back to the bar and ordered another drink. All other customers had left except two Ashcroft men. Bayard joined them, purely for alibi purposes. Every minute of his own time must be accounted for.

"Persistent cuss, Gus is," one of the Ashcroft men observed. "This makes the 'steenth time he's grubstaked a prospector. Nothin' to show for it yet, but he never gives up."

"Gus'll hit, one of these days. Law of averages. Like drawin' to an inside straight. You can't miss every time."

Bayard listened idly. He knew they were talking about an Ashcroft saloonman named Gus Gleason. Some called him Gus the Grubstaker. He was always trading a mule-load of grub for an interest in whatever claim the prospector might stake out while the grub lasted. Usually the period was sixty to ninety days.

"Who'd he grubstake this time, George?"

George furrowed his brow. "The name slips me just now, Harry. Some fella from Aspen. He'll try his luck at the head of Piney Creek, I understand, right above the *Montezuma*."

"The *Montezuma's* a Tabor property, ain't it?"

"It sure is. A grubstaked prospector found it, back in '81, and assigned it to Senator Tabor. If you'll check back you'll find that's the way Tabor got most of his high grade mines. Like the *Little Pittsburgh* at Leadville and the *Montezuma* and *Tam-O-Shanter* at Ashcroft. He's worth a sweet eight million right now, Tabor is, and never swung a pick in his life."

Harry held his drink to the light and nodded sagely. "So Gus Gleason figgers he can do the same thing, if he puts up enough grubstakes. Meantime he has to make a livin' dishin' up cheap whisky at Ashcroft."

"He was down here in Aspen not long ago," George remembered, "and got a bottle cracked over his head. Let loose with a couple of shots and they fined him fifty dollars."

"Have another one, gentlemen," Bayard invited. It was clear that they didn't think much of their fellow townsman, Gus the Grubstaker.

"Don't mind if we do," Harry said.

From a block north came a shrill whistle. Then another. Bayard heard running steps along the Cooper Avenue walk. "Sounds like police," George said. "Another saloon fight, maybe."

Harry nodded absently. "I just remembered that guy's name, George."

"What guy's name?"

"The fella that trailed up Piney Creek with Gleason's grubstake. He was headin' fer Telluride but Gus talked him into tryin' the high country above Ashcroft. Fella named Hostetter — What's the matter, Mister?"

Frank Bayard's glass crashed on the brass footrail. "Did you say Hostetter?"

"That's the name. Hostetter. Friend of yourn?"

Dizziness came over Bayard. Blood drained from his full blond face and for the moment he was too shocked to answer. Hostetter! The man was still here in Pitkin County! Not in faraway Telluride, beyond two sky-high ranges. He was barely twenty miles from Aspen and would be there for sixty days.

In that high, lonely spot he'd get no news, probably. But if he hit pay rock he'd come full speed to record a claim at the Aspen courthouse. And in sixty days, whether or not he struck a vein, snow would drive him down to Ashcroft or Aspen.

The bartender, setting out another drink, peered across the bar. "You ain't feelin' too good, are you, Mr. Bayard?"

Mechanically Bayard picked up the glass but he was still too dazed to answer. In either Ashcroft or Aspen Hostetter would hear talk. Talk of the boom at his old mine, the *Lost Friend*. A property he'd transferred to a stage driver named Brian. The cat would be out, then.

Losing a fortune wasn't what most frightened Bayard. Exposure meant prison. A Pitkin County court, with a jury of miners, would have small mercy.

He tossed down the liquor and let it fire his brain. Only one possible way out of it, he decided. He let the fire burn while he steeled his decision. Hostetter must be handled like Brian. He'd sent Lockwood to deal with Brian. Just as easily he could make Lockwood take care of Hostetter. A set-up, Hostetter, pecking rock all alone at the head of Piney. One bullet from an unseen rifleman would do it. Lockwood, bold enough to rob a stage, was just the man for it.

I sent him once and I can send him again. I can make him dance — or kill!

Again came a police whistle, this time from somewhere west of Monarch. Then a hack drew up at the Clarendon and a late reveller came in.

"Hear the latest?" Intense excitement painted the newcomer's face. "A killing over at Doc Coxon's," he reported. "Guy sneaked in and emptied his gun at a guy in bed."

The bartender was agog. "Who?"

"Remember that stage driver who got beat up the other day?"

"You don't say? Wes Brian! Always liked that boy. You say someone sneaked in and filled him full of lead?"

"No. Just the other way. The guy sneaked in, all right, and cut loose at the bed. But Wes wasn't in it. Wes only fired one shot himself."

"You mean it was the prowler got killed," prodded Harry from Ashcroft, "'stead of Brian?"

"You said it. If you're sending flowers, send 'em to Myron Lockwood."

No one could believe it except Bayard. Bayard gripped the bar tightly to keep from falling. He felt sick, beaten, hopeless. His cat's-paw was dead. Leaving

Brian more to be feared than ever. Tomorrow Brian would be the biggest headline in the county. His name might ring even to the remoteness of upper Piney Creek and reach Hostetter.

"Myron Lockwood!" the bartender gasped. "You can't mean *him!*"

"He's a high flyer, ain't he?" queried George.

"He was," the newcomer said. "But not any more. Right now he's just a corpse on the way to the morgue."

The barkeeper mopped his bar sadly. "That's the way it goes, here around Aspen. Today you're up and tomorrow you're down."

"Ain't it the truth?" agreed Harry from Ashcroft.

Of them all, no one knew it better than Frank Bayard.

The coroner's inquest the next afternoon could have only one outcome. Bayard attended it. He sat at the back of the room and listened nervously. Every inch of standing space was occupied and a curious crowd filled the walk outside. Gun play wasn't uncommon in Aspen. But no shooting had ever been as sensational as this one.

Not far from Bayard, solemn and tense, stood Joshua B. Wilbur. Revulsion darkened the financier's broad, grim face. As he listened, alternate shock and relief registered there. Shock at the sudden exposure of Lockwood; relief that it had come in time to save Phyllis from a tragic mistake.

A parade of witnesses took the stand. Doctor Coxon, Alfredo, patients from rooms five and six, the Hopkins

Street patrolman. The patrolman summed it up. "He sneaked in and fired four times at what looked like a man in bed. Then twice at a man's voice. Bullet holes prove it. At the sixth shot, Brian fired and made a hit."

A bullet-riddled pillow quickly convinced the jurymen. Beyond any possible doubt Myron Lockwood had entered stealthily to kill a sleeper in the dark.

Doctor Snow, the coroner, asked one more question. "But why?"

Only Wesley Brian could answer that. With his head still bandaged, Wes took the stand and was sworn.

"A week ago Monday," he reminded them, "a masked man held up my stage. I figured it was Lockwood."

A dropping pin could have been heard. Doctor Snow broke the silence. "What made you think so?"

In simple words Wes gave his reasons. "It's not proof," he admitted, "so I didn't tell the sheriff. All I did was ask Lockwood how come he got that whip-cut on his ear. He said it was a thorn scratch. But he knew I was on to him. I guess that's why he tried to gun me."

The jury came to a verdict without leaving the room. Lockwood's death, it said, had occurred while he was committing a crime, and was justified by the law of self defense.

Frank Bayard pushed his way out. At the sidewalk a man behind him tapped his shoulder. He turned to confront the bitterly disillusioned Joshua Wilbur. "Will you do something for me, Bayard?"

"Anything at all, Mr. Wilbur."

"Go to Colonel Willard's stable and reserve a private conveyance to Leadville. A closed carriage and his best horses. We'd like to leave at once from the Clarendon."

"Yes, Mr. Wilbur. You'll be coming back, I hope?"

"As soon," the financier promised grimly, "as I can put Phyllis on a train for New York. One other thing, Bayard. Ten days ago Lockwood gave me a check for twenty-five hundred dollars. It was on the First National of Leadville. Later he bought it back with cash and tore it up."

"I was there when he did it," Bayard remembered.

"What about that check? Would it have bounced?"

"I don't know, Mr. Wilbur. While you're in Leadville, why don't you ask the bank?"

"I will." Joshua B. Wilbur stalked resolutely off toward the Clarendon.

Bayard ordered the carriage and was watching from the bar when it drew up at the hotel. Phyllis Wilbur, wearing a travelling cloak and veil, went out to it with her father. Goodbyes would only embarrass her so Bayard kept his distance. She hadn't even told the Normans she was leaving.

Bayard watched the carriage, with its curtains drawn, roll away toward Independence Pass and Leadville. It would take the rest of today and all night to get there. He felt sorry for Phyllis. She was running away from an unbearable humiliation. For weeks she'd allowed her name to be linked with Lockwood's. No wonder Joshua Wilbur was packing her off to New York.

Then Bayard saw Wesley Brian turn into the hotel. In the last hour the bandage had been removed from his bruised and cut face. He had a do-or-die look as he came into the lobby. Bayard edged a bit closer and heard him say to the clerk, "I'd like to see Miss Norman, please."

"Wait in the parlor, Mr. Brian, and I'll tell her you're here." A deference in the clerk's voice meant that Wes Brian had become a celebrity since his battle with a killer last night.

Bayard easily guessed his errand. Wes Brian had agreed to buy a Cattle Creek farm on two conditions. He must settle his score with a stage robber; and he must square himself with Honora. The first was done. He was attending to the second matter now.

It suited Bayard. The sooner it was done the sooner he'd get Brian out of Pitkin County.

A bellboy came down the stairs, followed by Honora. The girl disappeared into the hotel's small parlor.

It wouldn't take long, Bayard thought. Either she'd forgive him at once or she wouldn't at all. Most likely she would. A girl naturally feels sympathy toward a boy who's been beaten up in one room and shot at in another.

Bayard waited through another highball, watching the lobby for Brian to cross it and be gone.

A half hour slipped by and Wes didn't come out of the parlor. It disturbed Bayard. He had his own plans for Honora. Wes Brian was much nearer her age than Bayard. Not a bad looking kid, the broker admitted. All the more reason to get him far off from Aspen.

Bayard went restlessly into the lobby and took a seat as near as he dared to the parlor door. It stood slightly ajar and he heard voices. Wes Brian's had a lilt. "I'm sure glad you're not sore at me any more."

A distinct remorse was in Honora's. "I'm sorry I was rude to you, that day."

"You'll be headin' east pretty soon?"

"Just as soon as father testifies in a trial. And thanks for sending me that warning by Mr. Random. The sheriff has a special guard posted, in case Jenner's friends come around. What are *your* plans, Mr. Brian?"

"You make me feel kinda old, callin' me that. Most folks call me Wes. Me? I'm buyin' a little stock ranch about forty miles below here. Just above Glenwood Springs. It's got a cottonwood creek on it, and a three-room log cabin, and . . ."

Bayard couldn't catch it all. The voices were low, intimate, and gave him a sense of being shut out. He went back to the bar for a drink.

When next he looked into the lobby Honora and Brian were crossing it. At the door the girl stopped to say goodbye. Wes Brian took her hand and it seemed to Bayard he held it a damnably long time. The boy's face was lighted up, and so was the girl's. It seemed to Bayard that a spark passed between them. She'd never looked at *him* like that.

He moved nearer and caught one final word. "Would you let me write to you, some time? I'd sure like to."

"Of course you may," Honora said. With that consent Wes Brian went whistling down the walk.

CHAPTER
TEN

In the morning Bayard waited in his Galena Street office. Brian would be coming in to close the deal for a Cattle Creek quarter-section. Fretfully Bayard wished it was a hundred miles to Cattle Creek, instead of only forty. But at least it was out of the mining belt. People down that way never heard of the *Lost Friend* mine. Their world was bounded on four sides by grass and cows and hay and horses.

A few clients came in, but not Wesley Brian. Mr. Cowenhoven's bookkeeper wanted to invest his savings in shares of the *Little Annie*. Henry Tourtelotte, just down from the Park, dropped by for the latest quotation on silver. "One dollar and six cents per ounce," Bayard told him.

Then a committee of ladies called to sell tickets for a *Bal Masque* at the Rink. Gambling that Honora would go with him, Bayard bought two.

It was nearly noon when his superintendent at the *Lost Friend* came in.

"Shaping up better than ever," Harv Random reported. "Assays keep running consistently around eight hundred ounces of silver per ton. By the end of the week we'll have round-the-clock shifts."

Bayard licked his lips. "How many tons per day can you take out?"

"Not so many right at first. But when I get the new hoist machinery operating and a few more hauling teams lined up, we'll move seventy tons every twenty-four hours. The first ten tons will pay overhead, freight and smelting charges. After that it's velvet. Sixty tons net profit per day." The engineer grinned broadly. "Figure it out yourself, Mr. Bayard."

Bayard did, on a scratch pad, and the result made him gasp. On the basis of current assays and the current market for silver, the *Lost Friend's* net profit would run about five thousand dollars per day. Three-fifths of it would be Bayard's. In less than a year it would bring him a cool million.

"Keep up the good work, Random. I'll report this, of course, to the minority stockholders at Leadville."

Elation fired Bayard's face but faded before the engineer was more than out of sight. Only two men could spoil this for him and one of them, Wes Brian, was reining a calico horse to a stop in front. The rider dismounted, dropped the reins, loosened the cinch of a handsome, silver-trimmed saddle, then came with clinking spurs into Bayard's office.

"Jim Downing looked up the title for me. It's okay. And I ran into an old bunkie who's seen the place. It's a good buy, he says. So make out the papers, Frank."

Bayard promptly signed a title and made Wes Brian sign a note. "There you are. The down payment's already in my safe. Where did you get that good looking calico?"

"A gift from the stage company," Wes told him. "When I went in to resign my drivin' job, they had him all saddled and ready."

Bayard wasn't much surprised. Carson had always been more than fair with his drivers. He'd be especially grateful to this one for taking care of a stage robber.

"You'll need a loan to stock the place," Bayard offered. "So I'll give you a letter to the Glenwood Springs bank . . ."

"You needn't bother," Wes broke in. "Seems like this is my lucky day. Can't understand why everybody wants to make a fuss over me. Mr. Lyster of the First National just called me in and handed me a thousand bucks." Wes waved a cashier's check for that sum. "Said a client of the bank wants me to have it for nailing Lockwood. Didn't say who the client is."

Bayard could easily guess. The client would be Joshua B. Wilbur. By exposing Lockwood, this boy had saved the Wilburs from a scandalous entanglement.

"You'll buy livestock with it?"

Wes nodded. "I'll start with twenty heifers and a wagon team. They tell me I can borrow a mowin' machine from a neighbor. Grass is stirrup-high along Cattle Creek, they say. So I'm off to put up some winter feed. So long, Frank."

Wes went out and swung aboard the calico. Bayard stood in the doorway to see him off.

"One other thing, Frank. I got a ten dollar bet posted at the Buckhorn bar. If the Midland beats the narrow gauge into town, collect it for me, will you? And mail it to me at the ranch?"

"I'll do that," Bayard promised. With a sense of relief he watched Wes Brian lope the calico down Galena and at Main Street turn west on the Glenwood road.

Walking slowly to the Clarendon, Bayard tried to feel good about it. Brian was gone now, and might never show up here again.

Still, a hard fact remained and it nagged Bayard. That boy was the true owner of thirty thousand shares in the *Lost Friend*. If the truth ever came out, the fortune would go to Brian and Bayard would go to prison.

There could be no real security, Bayard worried, as long as two dangers hung over him. John Hostetter and Wesley Brian.

In the Clarendon dining room he joined Honora and her father. "What's this about the Wilburs?" the Major asked him. "Are they coming back?"

"Mr. Wilbur is. But not Phyllis."

"What a shame!" Honora exclaimed. She'd become fond of Phyllis Wilbur.

A man at a nearby table was a sheriff's deputy. His room was across the hall from Roger Norman's. Bayard wondered if the Major knew he was being guarded.

"By the way, Honora, I picked up tickets for the *Bal Masque*. You'll go, won't you?"

"If it's before the tenth," the girl agreed. "We're leaving on the eleventh, you know."

When Frank Bayard got back to his office his spirits were up again. Honora hadn't mentioned Wesley Brian and no doubt she'd soon forget him. She'd go east — a thousand miles to St. Louis. But when a man has a million dollars a thousand miles needn't bother him. He'd follow Honora there and lay the world at her feet.

Bayard opened his office door and went in. A customer was waiting and his cocky pose annoyed the broker. The man sat with his feet propped impudently on the desk.

"Howdy, Frank." The man grinned, pushed his hat back on a half bald head and then Bayard remembered him.

Gus Gleason. Gus the Grubstaker, who ran a second rate bar and a brace faro bank at Ashcroft.

"What can I do for you, Gleason?"

"It ain't what you can do for me, Frank." An eyelid drooped slyly. "It's what I can do for you."

An ugly fact jolted Bayard. He remembered talk at the Clarendon bar, night before last. About Gleason grubstaking Hostetter!

Bayard sank heavily into his swivel chair. He tried to keep his voice calm. "You mean some pick-and-shovel burro man of yours hit pay rock?"

"It's a heap better than that, Frank. His name's Hostetter and I don't give a damn whether he hits pay rock or not. I'm gonna get mine the easy way. Because what he told me as he headed up Piney Creek is money in the bank. Silver in the mint! Bullion at the smelter!"

A sense of impending doom weighed on Bayard. "What did he tell you?"

"He said he sold his *Lost Friend* stock to a stage skinner named Brian. He said he'd just writ Brian a letter tellin' about a soft stope roof. Then he trailed up Piney. Next day the Aspen stage rolled in with the latest copy of the *Times*. Your name was in a headline, Frank. Not Brian's, but yours."

Playing innocent wouldn't work and Bayard knew it. The man had him. One whisper would send lawyers up Piney Creek to find Hostetter and ask him questions. And right now Wes Brian was the pet of the town. Everyone was on his side because of the Lockwood fracas. Jim Downing, the best lawyer on the west slope, had just checked a title for him.

With his face the dead gray color of lead Bayard went to his office door and locked it. He pulled down the blinds and sat facing Gleason. The man wore a gun. He was a practised gunman and Bayard wasn't.

"What do you want?"

"A third of your net take, Frank."

A third of his net take, Bayard calculated, would top a thousand dollars a day when full production got under way. "Don't be ridiculous. I'd see you in hell first."

"Where from?" Gleason parried. "From Canon City?" The state penitentiary was at Canon City.

"Sending me to prison won't get you a cent."

"You can stay out of it and still be rich. I've looked up the assays."

"I might give you ten percent," Bayard haggled.

"You'll give me thirty-three percent."

"And if I don't?"

"Then the whole town'll know the truth by sundown. Including the county judge, the D.A. and Jim Downing."

100

The pressure was on and Bayard squirmed. His mind groped desperately and could see only one way out. A third split to this blackmailer wouldn't be so bad if it took out all other hazards.

"It's a lot of money, Gleason. You'd have to earn it."

The half bald gambler cocked an eye. "Yeh? How do I earn it?"

Bayard glanced significantly at Gleason's gun. "Two men can put the skids under us. They don't know it yet. They don't even know each other. But if they ever get together the whole thing's not worth a penny to either of us."

Gleason narrowed his eyes shrewdly. "I see what you mean, pardner. You want me to shut 'em up. For keeps. That way I earn my cut."

Bayard winced and lowered his voice. "Not so loud, please."

Gus Gleason took a stogie from his vest and struck a match on the mahogany desk. Contempt shaded his words. "You haven't got the nerve to do it yourself, have you, Frank?"

It was true and Bayard couldn't deny it. He could plan murder but there wasn't enough iron in him to pull a trigger himself. By subtle suggestion he'd sent Lockwood to kill Brian. Now, by blunt talk and a cold cash trade, he must send Gleason to kill both Brian and Hostetter.

"I know where one of 'em is," Gleason said. "Where's the other?"

"After today he'll be in a cabin on Cattle Creek. Three miles above where it comes into Roaring Fork."

Gleason sucked on the stogie. His mouth made an O as he blew smoke rings. "Why can't we leave him out of it? He'll never know anything except through Hostetter."

Bayard had tried to tell himself the same thing. But he wasn't quite sure of it. If he must pay out a third of the net take, he might as well get his money's worth. The worst danger was Hostetter, but Brian alone might still make trouble.

"Hostetter wrote him a letter," Bayard argued. "Brian showed it to friends and none of them can explain it. It doesn't make sense — except by one answer. The right one. Some day Brian might get smart and figure it out."

"With Hostetter dead, he'd only be guessing."

"But it would put him on the right track. He'd go to Ashcroft where Hostetter wrote the letter. He'd talk to everyone who saw Hostetter there. If Hostetter told *you* what happened, maybe he told somebody else too. Somebody at a bar; a waitress; some wagoneer he passed on the road. If Brian finds anyone like that . . ."

"It would only be hearsay," Gleason insisted.

"But with it he could make me bring that certificate into court. Brian's name was in ink. Under a glass the erasure shows. Brian's name was in Hostetter's writing; now mine's in mine. But with both Brian and Hostetter out of the way, there'd never be any close inspection like that."

For the first time a grudging respect gleamed from Gleason's eyes. "I see you've figured out everything, Frank."

"Well?"

"When you lay it on the line like that," Gleason admitted, "I don't have much choice. If I tell on you, I get nothing. If I don't tell on you and Hostetter does, I still get nothing. If neither I nor Hostetter nor Brian tell on you, I can book passage for Europe along with all the other silver kings." Gus the Grubstaker chuckled. "And you too, Frank. Maybe we'll meet at some bar in Paris."

"You'll do it, then?"

Again Gleason blew thoughtful smoke rings. "I could keep a long way off and use a rifle," he murmured, thinking aloud. "Hostetter first, then Brian." He got up, took a hitch at his gunbelt and moved toward the door. There he turned and shot a mean look. "But I'll save one bullet, pardner."

Bayard blinked. "Who for?"

"For you — if you try a double cross."

CHAPTER
ELEVEN

By sundown Wes made Frying Pan City, where the Frying Pan River joined Roaring Fork, and where the Midland Railroad would soon turn the corner to head upvalley toward Aspen. Already Wes had passed grading camps on both sides of the valley, the Midland grade on one side and the Rio Grande on the other. Neither road would have its rails here for more than a month yet. Bridges and tunnels, not the grading of roadbeds, were the construction limitations.

Grading crews and the parasites preying on them had made Frying Pan City a place of tents and unpainted board fronts, new and raw and lawless. It wouldn't last long, Wes thought. Construction camps never did. A few months of dust-choked life, of brawls and sprees, and these tents would move on.

Right now there were three plank stores. One of them had rooms above it and a stable for transient horses. Wes put up his calico and took a room. He heard gunshots up the street and no one seemed to pay any attention. "You got any law here?" he asked a waitress who served him supper.

"Take a look over in the Big Tent," the girl said, "and judge for yourself."

As he finished eating a committee of three citizens approached Wes.

"You're Wesley Brian of Aspen?" the spokesman asked. Wes admitted it.

"My name's Horner. These are Ed Winch and Otto Schultz. We own the three stores. We're the main taxpayers."

"We read about you in the *Times*," Winch put in. "About how you shot it out with a stage robber."

"So ve vant to offer you a chob," Schultz said bluntly.

"What kind of a job?"

"Town marshal," Horner said. "We need one bad. The town's full of toughs and they drive away all decent trade."

"We'll pay a hundred dollars a month," Winch pleaded.

It was more than he'd ever earned as a stage driver and Wes was tempted. As he hesitated, another shot rang out from the Big Tent Saloon. "That's the way it goes all the time," Horner said. "We're right on the line between Pitkin and Garfield counties and neither sheriff pays us any mind."

"Top of that," Winch added, "we're right on the line between the mine country and the cow country, so we get the backwash of both. Every night a thousand graders come in to blow their pay. Do the decent stores get any of it? No. Just the *honkytonks*."

"The Ike Buford gang rode in today," Horner fretted. "Shootin' off their mouths and guns, as usual. Nobody to stop 'em."

"Unless *you* do," Winch amended. He held a brass star toward Wes. "You can start in right now."

It was hard to say no. Hard because they'd think he was afraid. But Wes had other plans and he stuck to them.

"Sorry. You'll have to get somebody else." With a shrug he brushed by the committee and went up to bed.

He was sleeping soundly when Colonel Rolfe Clemson rode in from his ranch up the Frying Pan. The colonel, newly arrived from Kentucky, had just bought the place and planned to raise race horses on it. His black frock coat, his thin, richly veined face and his spiked goatee made him look more like a planter than a ranchman. A white-haired Negro followed him on a mule.

Colonel Clemson stopped at the post office for his mail.

"Stage is late," he was told. "Mail won't be in for an hour yet."

"Wait here for it, Ezra," Clemson directed his servant. "Then bring it to me at Mr. Horner's store."

Riding on toward the Horner store the colonel had to pass the Big Tent. Three men swaggered out of it and one of them pushed a gun into the Kentuckian's ribs. The man had a whisky voice. "Get down off that bronc; then come in and stand treat."

Clemson had a gun of his own in an inside breast pocket. He looked from face to face of these rowdies and decided not to use it. "If you insist." His

106

compliance was softly courteous as he stepped from the saddle.

Ike Buford prodded him into the tent. Hanging lanterns made light for it. The bar was long planks laid across saw horses. Customers were the scum of the grading camps. "Your pleasure, gentlemen," the colonel invited.

A bartender poured whiskies for the crowd. "See'f he's got a gun, Jakey," Buford yelled. "And you stand right back of him, Peck, in case he gets funny."

Colonel Clemson didn't get funny. He made no resistance when Jakey took the breast pocket pistol and slid it down the bar to Ike Buford.

"Let's see if it shoots!" Buford took aim at the tent's only decoration, which was a gold fish bowl at the far end of the bar. The gun boomed, the glass shattered, and small red fish wriggled on the sawdust floor. Everyone laughed except the colonel and the bartender.

"Set 'em up again!" Ike demanded, waving both his own gun and the colonel's.

"You heard him," Peck growled. He stood back of Clemson with a cocked gun.

Clemson didn't argue. Again he treated the crowd. And again. In all he paid for seven rounds. The cocked gun behind him frightened him more than Buford. For Peck was drunk and Buford wasn't. He could hear clicks as Peck kept cocking and uncocking the hammer with his thumb. Between rounds Buford jeered at him. "Now I'm gonna plug you anyhow." He kept aiming at Clemson's head, hoping to make the colonel beg or crawl. All evening he'd lorded it over the town, rough shod and reckless, and every laugh from the bar flies swelled his sense of importance.

At each demand the colonel complied with quiet courtesy.

After the seventh round an old Negro came in with a dozen letters. "Your mail, suh." He handed them to his master.

Ike Buford snatched the letters and threw them on the floor. The Negro blinked down at them for a moment. Then he stooped, picked up the letters and brushed sawdust from them. "Whatcha doin' with my mail, old man?" Buford fixed bloodshot eyes on the servant. "Just for that you can hold 'em out for targets."

Amid maudlin cheers from the bar flies he made Ezra stand at one end of the tent and hold a letter at arm's length. From ten paces away Ike Buford sent a bullet through it. "Okay. Hold out another'n."

Every hit drew cheers.

Five envelopes, one by one, were shot from the Negro's shaking hand. Ike was aiming at the sixth when a voice spoke from the tent's entrance. "What's goin' on in here? A bear hunt?"

Wesley Brian stood there, at first more curious than angry. "You fellas made so much noise I couldn't sleep."

Then he saw a frock-coated Southerner and beyond him a panic-stricken Negro. A challenge from Buford told him the rest. "You want to make something of it, Mister?"

There were three of them, one of them drunk with power and the other two with whisky. All three had

108

guns and were itching for trouble. A quick surprise attack was Wes Brian's only chance and he fired from the hip. He fired three times in a breath. The gun never left his holster, which had an open bottom, and which swung in a short arc between each pair of shots.

The first broke Ike Buford's arm and the second plowed Peck's scalp, dropping Peck to his knees with a howl. Jakey fired a whisper too late; a bullet through the shoulder spun him against the bar.

Only Peck went down. But the other two stood gunless, pain-frozen. And instantly the crowd changed sides. A minute ago they were fawning on Buford. Now almost to a man they cheered Wes Brian. The bartender came out for a look and gathered up the guns. "You let 'em off too easy, young fella."

"Wrap 'em up," Wes said. "Or patch 'em up. I haven't got time to fool with 'em." He turned to the colonel. "You all right?"

Clemson smiled ruefully. "And properly grateful," he said. "It will be my high privilege if I may return this service, some day. My card, sir."

The card was in Wes Brian's pocket at daybreak when he rode on down Roaring Fork. He'd made one new friend; and three deadly enemies. "The more I see of track camps, Patch," he told the calico, "the more I like cowboys and miners."

Seventeen miles below Frying Pan he came to the mouth of a creek flowing in from the northeast. Cottonwoods lined it, with an underbrush of wild cherry and plum. Wes turned up it with an eager suspense. "This here's Cattle Creek, Patch. Home Sweet Home'll be loomin' any minute."

The creek valley was a rich meadow bottom with a homestead cabin about every half mile. But the cabins he passed were empty. The homesteaders, Wes guessed, had hired out with their teams to the grading contractors.

Three miles upcreek he came to a gate. The grass beyond hadn't been grazed this summer; in spots it was stirrup high. "Your winter rations, Patch." With a throb of pride Wes opened the gate.

This filing was a "long quarter" — a mile long by a quarter mile wide. Just wide enough to span the bottomland. Timbered hills on either side were open, public range. The land adjoining upcreek was a large ranch, the Circle Cross. Wes knew an exstage driver, Ray Plover, who was now punching cows for the Circle Cross. "We're in beef country, Patch. Down this way they wouldn't know a stope from a shaft."

The cabin, near the quarter-section's upstream end, had log walls, a rock chimney and a shingled gable. A shed, corral, well and two and a half miles of four-wire fence! Again a question puzzled Wes. Why had Frank Bayard sold him the place so cheap, and for such a small payment down?

Jubilation chased away puzzlement as Wes dismounted in front of the first home he'd ever owned. What more could a man want? A good house on good land, a good saddle on a good horse — and a thousand dollar check in his pocket. All he needed now was . . .

Almost guiltily he thought of Honora Norman. Would she like it here? There'd be lupine and clematis along the creek, wild roses in the meadow. What would it be like, if he rode up some day and saw her open that door?

August ended and a week of September slipped by. Wes Brian worked from sun to sun as he'd never worked before.

Most of his money was gone. But he had plenty to show for it. He'd registered a brand and it was burned on the flanks of twenty White-face heifers grazing on government land just outside his fence.

He'd bought a stout bay team, with wagon and harness, but the mower he was riding now was borrowed from the Circle Cross. They'd been right neighborly, thanks to Ray Plover up there.

"Giddap." The sickle clattered as Wes made circle after circle. Thirty acres of his best grass lay in swaths. Tomorrow he'd return the mower and borrow a sulky rake.

At sundown he drove to the cabin and put up the team. Ray Plover on his way upcreek today had dropped off some mail. Wes looked hopefully for a letter from Honora but there wasn't any. He'd written her buoyantly about the beauties of his ranch.

Nothing but a seed catalogue and a copy of the Aspen *Times*. There'd be a *Bal Masque* at the Rink, the *Times* said, on the night of September eighth. Wes glanced at his wall calendar. Today was the eighth.

CHAPTER
TWELVE

Mrs. McLaughlin, hostess at the Clarendon, kneeled beside Honora with a mouthful of pins. She gave a last deft touch here and loosened a bow there. "Now put on your mask, dear. Isn't she beautiful, Major?"

Major Norman nodded proudly as Honora put on her mask. The girl stretched out her arms and whirled about, swirling her ruffled skirts. "I'm Spanish Lady, Dad. I wanted to be Alsatian Lady but Genevieve Sweetser spoke for it first."

"Ella Chatfield will be Greek Lady," Mrs. Mac chattered. "Emma Strait's Lady Fireman and Mrs. Doctor Perry is Yachtswoman."

"Hold on!" the Major protested. "If every woman in town knows what every other woman will wear, what's the use of masks?"

"They're just to fool the men," Honora explained gayly.

"Yours is waiting in the lobby," the hostess reminded, "so hurry down."

Honora kissed her father, picked up her fan and swept out to the night's adventure. This would be her last party in Aspen. The Jenner trial was only two days away; then they'd catch a stage east.

Mrs. Mac followed to the head of the stairs from where she could see Frank Bayard waiting in the lobby. She called back over her shoulder, "They'll be the handsomest couple on the floor, Major."

Roger Norman had no doubt of it. Left alone, he went through the connecting door to his own room. Today's *Times* was on the bed and he read restlessly for a while. President Moffat of the D & R G, it said, would arrive with his chief engineer tomorrow. And Sheriff Hooper was still away with the Aspen militia fighting Colorow and his Utes.

At ten o'clock the Major prepared for bed. When he was in his night shirt, he opened the window for fresh air.

The window gave to Durant Street. And something with an oddly familiar shape lay on the outer sill. Right where he'd be sure to see it when he raised the sash at bedtime. Sight of it excited the Major, set his nerves to jumping and jangling. He didn't stop to speculate why the thing was there.

But there it lay! A half pint! And bedtime had always been his worst daily crisis. Then most of all he needed a drink.

Roger Norman whetted his lips, looked guiltily at the transom over his door. They thought he didn't know about a bodyguard in a room across the hall. For days he'd known the man was there.

The Major didn't touch the bottle until he'd turned out the light. Then he took the whisky and sat on the bed with it. Just this one little half pint wouldn't hurt him. Only a nightcap. Then he'd go to sleep. He'd promised Honora . . . but she need never know about this little short one. She was out having a good time herself, wasn't she?

He uncorked the bottle and upended it to his lips. He let the liquor trickle deliciously down his throat. He needed this. It was a lifesaver after he'd been penned up like a spoiled boy for two long weeks, with nothing but creek water and milk.

Major Norman sipped again, slowly and stingily. He made the half pint last nearly an hour. The room was dark. Even if the guard peeked through the transom he wouldn't see anything.

When the bottle was empty, the Major threw it out the window. He heard it plop in the dust of Durant Street. Then he lay down to sleep — but couldn't. Devils nagged him. He tossed and twisted. His thirst was primed now. It was torture to cut a man off with a mere taste like that.

He sat up and reached for his clothes. With his nerves thumping he dressed in the dark. But when he got to the door he was afraid to open it. That cursed guard might have his own door open, right across the hall.

If so the man could see the Major's door but he couldn't see Honora's. So Roger Norman slipped stealthily into his daughter's room. Then he remembered he didn't have any money. Keeping him without money was one way they'd made sure he didn't go out to a bar.

But Honora had money. She hadn't taken her purse to the ball with her. Roger Norman groped through a

114

dresser drawer till he found it. All he took was one silver dollar. Enough to buy a pint. He'd bring the pint back to his room and they'd never know he'd been out.

He opened the door to a crack and peered warily into the hall. An open door ten steps to his right was the door of the guard's room. The man might be sitting up in the dark, watching. But he couldn't see around a corner. Roger Norman tip-toed out and turned the other way, toward rear stairs. By using them he wouldn't need to cross the lobby.

The back stairs let him out into a hitch lot full of tethered teams. Mostly they were carriage teams which had brought people to the ball. Monarch Street ran along the west side of the lot with the brilliantly lighted Rink on the Cooper Avenue corner. Orchestra music came twanging from it.

Saloon Row lay to the east, so Norman slipped among the carriages to Mill Street, scurried across it to an alley running eastward back of the *Comique*. This alley would come out on Hunter Street and there he could dodge into the Corner Saloon by its rear door.

Roger Norman was almost to it, running fast, when a foot reached out and tripped him. As he sprawled in the dust a sack was inverted over his head. Strings pulled tightly about his throat choked off his cry. Then two men made off with him, one holding his kicking legs and the other his sacked head.

At three in the morning a frantic knocking awakened Deputy Sheriff Hearn. He hit the floor, one hand reaching for his pants and the other for his gun. "It's

Dad! He's gone. Hurry!" The distressed voice from the hall was Honora Norman's.

When the bodyguard joined her she led him through her own room and into her father's. The bed was empty. An open window hadn't quite dispelled an odor of whisky. Hearn turned grimly to the girl. "Look and see if he took any money."

She went for a look at her purse. "There were some bills and a silver dollar. Only the dollar is gone." She was still dressed as Spanish Lady, in formal black with elbow-length sleeves and with a feathered fan dangling from her wrist. Her face was bloodless. "I shouldn't have left him!" she said wretchedly.

"Don't fret too much. I'll have him back here in no time," Hearn promised.

He went out, sure he'd find the Major in one of the town's twenty-seven saloons. The dollar wouldn't go far. But there were plenty who'd stand treat.

Neither the night clerk nor the Clarendon bartender had seen the Major, so Hearn rushed hotfoot to the courthouse. A deputy there dashed off to enlist McEvoy's crew while Hearn hurried east along Cooper, inquiring at bar after bar.

By four o'clock a dozen men were beating the town for Roger Norman. Not one of his old haunts had seen him. "Pick up Fred and Gil Dillon," Gavitt ordered. Sheriff Hooper was away with the militia and Gavitt was the ranking deputy.

"I'll put my force on it too," McEvoy said. Dawn of September Ninth was breaking. And tomorrow Alf Jenner's trial would open at the courthouse.

"Without Norman's testimony we can't convict," Gavitt predicted. "He was the only one who actually saw Jenner shoot that bartender. So the Dillons grabbed him. If we find him, we'll find him dead."

McEvoy nodded. "They're buddies of Jenner. No witness, no conviction."

By breakfast time the last doubt faded. Neither Fred nor Gil Dillon could be found. Yesterday they'd called at the jail to see Jenner, talking to him through the bars. Later Gil had been seen buying a half pint at the Abbey bar. The brand was Maid of the Nile. An empty half pint bottle of that brand was found in Durant Street opposite Roger Norman's open window.

By noon fifty men were out looking for the Major. Only a few expected to find him alive. Roaring Fork was dragged a mile each way from the town. Flares were dropped into a dozen deserted shafts, in fearful search for a battered body at the bottom. Couriers were dispatched at breakneck speed to block every pass. Taylor Pass toward St. Elmo; Pearl Pass toward Gunnison; Independence Pass toward Leadville and Granite; Hunter Pass toward the new Hagerman tunnel; or down Roaring Fork toward Glenwood Springs. To escape from Pitkin County, the Dillons would almost surely go by one of those five routes.

"Bring 'em back — dead or alive!" was Gavitt's blunt order. He'd already given up hope of saving Norman.

From her room window, Honora stared bitterly out at the town. She hated it and all its works; and right now she hated herself. Almost she hated Frank Bayard for taking her to the ball. If she'd stayed at home her father would still be with her. She'd deserted him right at the crisis, when he'd needed her most.

Frank Bayard had called twice to comfort her. She was inconsolable. When someone knocked she supposed it was Bayard again. But it was only a bellboy with today's *Times*. Honora looked at the headlines. The kidnapping of a murder witness had driven even the railroad race off the front page. Editor Wheeler was making a *cause célèbre* out of it.

"District Attorney Elder," she read, "has asked for a postponement. He wants time to find his only eye-witness, Roger Norman. The defense objects, demanding that the case be heard on schedule. If it is, and if Major Norman fails to appear, Jenner's acquittal is almost certain."

If! The word brought a shiver to Honora. It ran all through the news story and was on every lip in town. *If* the witness is alive . . . *If* he's found dead . . .

The day passed and a new one dawned. September Tenth, trial day for Alf Jenner! A packed courtroom listened to the heated debate between opposing counsel. The state pleaded for a week's postponement; the defense demanded no delay at all. A hundred eyes fixed balefully on Alf Jenner and made fear shadow his face.

Already there were whispers about how to handle Jenner, if the court should fail to convict. In all the seven years of its history Aspen had never seen a lynching. "Just the same," a man muttered to Frank

Bayard in the back row, "I'd hate to be Jenner if they turn him loose."

Judge Withers tried to be fair. He gave a little to each side and granted a two day postponement. "Court adjourned till the twelfth," he ruled. "We'll try the case then, witness or no witness."

Bayard elbowed his way out and crossed to the Brick Saloon. As he pushed through the swinging half-doors he bumped into a man coming out. Gus Gleason of Ashcroft!

For a moment the two stood face to face in the doorway, Bayard gaping, Gleason with a sly, twisted smile.

"Well?" Bayard asked huskily.

"I'm half done," Gleason reported. He drooped an eyelid, looked shiftily over his shoulder, then brushed by Bayard to a horse at the rack.

The horse had a rifle in its saddle scabbard. The Ashcroft man swung a leg over it and was off at a gallop.

Bayard, a shade paler, went on into the bar. He really needed a drink now. *Half done? Which half? Hostetter or Brian?*

CHAPTER
THIRTEEN

His face bronzed and perspiring, Wesley Brian stood on the hay wagon and punched his pitchfork into the wagon's last forkful of cured *vega*. He heaved it to the top of a stack he'd made on the roof of his shed. It was only a five-ton stack but it would get him through the winter. He looked proudly at a long, golden mound neatly rounded on top, covering the shed from end to end.

He climbed up there with his fork and trimmed the top. This mown meadow grass had lain two days in the windrow and the smell of it was sweet. He'd already hoisted up three twenty-foot wires, each with a cedar post tied to the ends. These weighted wires he draped across the stack at the quarter points, as insurance against high winds.

Poised there on the stack, he took off his hat to fan away sweat. A tough week's work, putting up this jag of feed all by himself. First he'd borrowed a mower, then a rake, then a hay frame for his wagon. This afternoon he'd return the frame with thanks. Darned good neighbors, the Circle Cross.

Something whistled past his ear. He saw it kick dust a hundred yards out in the stubble of his meadow; then he heard it ricochet on.

A bullet?

Wes slid down the stack and landed on the wagon frame. From there he jumped to the ground and ran to his cabin. His saddle gun stood in a corner. He pumped a shell into the chamber and stepped warily outside.

The shot had come from the east side of the valley, beyond the creek. A slope there was covered with dense oak brush. A man could get within two hundred yards of the cabin without being seen. Coming from upwind, with a noisy creek in between, the shot could be fired without Wes hearing it.

To save feed, Wes had turned his calico to pasture. Rounding it up would take too long. So he advanced grimly afoot, rifle at the ready, his eyes on the brushy slope beyond the creek. He could hardly doubt who the sniper was. He'd be one of the Ike Buford gang. No one else had it in for him except the Dillon brothers. And they'd already had their fun with him.

Wes waded the creek. The oak slope began directly at its east bank. Wes shifted to the left to get in line with his stack and the spot where a bullet had kicked dust. Then he moved cautiously up the hill.

Shortly he found sign. Boot marks. An empty rifle shell. And higher up, tracks where a shod horse had been tied in thick brush. After the miss, the sniper had made off uphill. The retreat bore south, in a direction which would strike Roaring Fork near Satank.

There the man would lose his sign in riffles. An hour's ride upstream from Satank would put him in Frying Pan City, stamping ground of the Buford gang.

Wes picked up the empty shell. It was a 44–40 UT cartridge. You hardly ever saw a UT shell any more. The UT factory had closed down more than a year ago. Nearly everyone used UMC or UX shells. As far as Wes knew, the Aspen and Glenwood Springs stores carried no other makes.

No use chasing that sniper. He'd be riding riffles before Wes could saddle a mount. Wes put the empty shell in his pocket and went back to the shed. He unharnessed and fed the wagon team. In the cabin he fired the stove and put a coffee pot on.

He was peeling potatoes when Ray Plover rode up.

Wes called to him, "Come and get it, neighbor."

Plover dropped his reins and dismounted. "Seein' as you're all through hayin', don't mind if I do." He came in and poured himself coffee.

Wes held up a brass rifle shell. "I just got shot at. Remember me tellin' you about Ike Buford? Either he or one of his playmates tossed a slug my way."

"When was that?"

Wes looked at his watch. "Just an hour ago. I was pattin' down the last forkful on my shed stack . . ."

"It wasn't Ike Buford," Plover broke in.

"Yeh? How do you know it wasn't?"

"Just an hour ago I saw him in Glenwood Springs. Him and his two side kicks. They were lined up on the walk watchin' Governor Alva Adams ride by. The governor's down there takin' personal command of the militia that's out fightin' the Utes."

"You saw all three of them? Buford, Peck and Jakey Runkle?"

122

"All three. Buford's got his arm in a sling. Must've been somebody else took a pot at you."

Wes rubbed his jaw thoughtfully. "Then it was Fred or Gil Dillon. They're the only other guys mad at me."

Ray Plover shook his head. "Guess again, Wes. It wasn't the Dillons, either. Read this and you'll know why." He was on his way home with the Circle Cross mail. In it was today's Glenwood Springs paper.

The latest sensation from Aspen was on the front page. Wes read the headlines and skimmed through the high lights.

"You're right, Ray. It wasn't the Dillon brothers. With posses beating the hills for them they wouldn't come by here just for a grudge shot."

"A stray shot from some hunter, maybe?"

"Not a chance. He missed me just that far." Wes held up a little finger. "Me on a haystack and him sniping from the brush. Know anyone who uses UT ammunition?"

Plover examined the empty shell, noting a factory mark on its cap end. "Been years since I've seen one of these UTs. Glenwood stores don't stock 'em any more. Where you goin', fella?"

Wes had spread a blanket on the floor. On it he tossed a slicker, an extra shirt and pair of socks, a tooth brush and towel — the bare minimum usually packed in a saddle roll.

"Do me a favor, Ray. Drive that hay frame back to the ranch with you. Then turn my team to pasture. I'm burnin' the breeze to Aspen."

Plover gaped. "It's forty miles to Aspen. What's the rush?"

"Friends of mine in trouble up there." Wes glanced again at a headline. KEY WITNESS KIDNAPPED. "I might be gone a week or two, Ray. Take a look at my heifers, will you, any time you pass by?"

Wes Brian went out, caught and saddled Patch.

Riding south over a ridge saved a mile or two. It was the direction taken by the sniper but Wes didn't waste time following tracks. He hit Roaring Fork just above the mouth of Rock Creek and turned easterly upstream. A forced ride should put him in Aspen by midnight. He must do what he could for Honora Norman.

"If her Dad's alive we've got to find him, Patch. And if he's not we'll make somebody hard to catch." He could hardly doubt that the Dillons had lured Norman from his room. By packing him off into the hills they'd keep him from testifying.

According to the news account, they'd postponed the Jenner trial from the tenth to the twelfth. Today was the twelfth. So the trial was going on right now. Wes Brian rarely spurred a horse. But he spurred this one and rode through Satank at a lope.

The calico was lathered when at sundown he drew up at a Frying Pan City feed shed. "Let him rest half an hour," he directed. "Then grain and water him." Wes made a round of the town's three stores. At each he showed an empty UT shell.

"We don't stock anything but UMCs," Horner said.

124

Otto Schultz and Ed Winch gave the same answer. Winch cocked a curious eye. "Whatsamatter? Did Ike Buford pay a call on you?"

"Not yet," Wes told him. "But somebody did. If you see anyone with a beltful of UT shells, let me know."

As light faded he called for his horse. At the feed shed a thin man with white hair and a goatee was saddling one of his own.

"Howdy, Colonel. Remember me?"

Colonel Clemson held out a hearty hand. "I'm not likely to forget. Come out to the ranch with me and spend the night."

"No time, Colonel. I'm hell-bent for Aspen." To give the calico another ten minutes' rest, Wes told the colonel why.

The Kentuckian frowned. "Looks like you're in for a lot of hard riding, son. A forced ride to Aspen and then you'll scour the hills for Norman. You can't do it right without a change of mounts." A practised eye told Clemson that the calico had already been ridden too hard. "See here, son. You'd better toss your saddle on mine and lead your own."

The offer astonished Wes. He looked at the colonel's mount — a blooded racer.

"What's mine's yours," Clemson insisted. "Name's Prince and he's fresh. Fresh and fast. Allow me, sir." He picked up Wes Brian's saddle and threw it on the back of his dappled chestnut racer. "Ride one and lead the other, turn about. You can cover lots of country, that way."

125

"Look, Colonel," Wes protested. "I'll be ridin' rough trails. High rocky ledges and brushy gulches. I'd get him all scuffed up."

"Nonsense. We both love horses; but we both know they were made to ride." The colonel's tone changed and his eyes twinkled. "It's four hours to Aspen. You mentioned a lady in distress up there. Where I came from we don't keep a lady waiting. Better get started, son."

"Not guilty!" The jury foreman announced the verdict with clear distaste. More than one juryman stared with undisguised contempt at the man on trial, Alf Jenner.

Yet the verdict could hardly be anything else. Only one person had witnessed the crime and that witness had failed to appear in court.

A sullen murmur went through the courtroom crowd. It chilled the elation on Jenner's face and made fear leak from his eyes. He was acquitted, but he still had to face the public opinion of Aspen.

The crowd parted to let him walk out. No hand touched him. People on the sidewalk stood back. A voice shouted, "He's guilty as hell!" But they let him go. Aspen, rough and ready and tough, had never yet staged a lynching.

Dark was creeping over the town when Jenner got to his old hotel, the Belmont House on East Cooper. "We're full up," the clerk said coldly.

Jenner tried the Thurman; then the Noble House on Hyman. Each had empty rooms, but neither would take him in. He was a pariah in Aspen, acquitted in court but convicted everywhere else. It wasn't merely because he'd killed a bartender. Bartenders were expendable in Aspen. But this man's guilt, in the eyes of the town, was linked with the guilt of Fred and Gil Dillon. The Dillons who'd lured a weak old man to his doom and brought heartache to a lovely young girl.

Alf Jenner went into the Fashion saloon but they wouldn't serve him. He tried the St. Charles on East Hopkins and was turned away. As he left the place a stone whizzed through the dark, barely missing him.

It would get worse as the night aged and Jenner knew it. Tonight men would toss liquor at twenty-seven bars with but one theme of talk. After each round resentment would grow louder, bolder. Bitter looks could lead to a flung stone and a stone could lead to a rope! Panic clutched at Jenner. He must get off the streets and hide.

Then he remembered Miranda. A young Mexicana who ran a cheap rooming house on the fringe of the Red Light district. Before his arrest Jenner had wined her a few times. He had an idea she liked him. He scurried around a corner and darted up Hunter Street toward Durant.

CHAPTER
FOURTEEN

Charley Barrow faced a street crowd, declaiming. He was spell-binding them. Brandy had painted florid streaks on his face. This was his fourth speech tonight and at each his rabble audience had grown bigger and angrier.

The Englishman himself wasn't too angry. But he liked applause. He liked to impress men with less schooling than himself and hear them cheer his smart phrases.

"What kind of a town is this, men?" he demanded. "A fiend kills in cold blood. When we jail him, his friends kidnap and murder the only witness. Now the fiend walks in our midst, a free man, laughing at us. Shall we let him get away with it?"

"No." The answer bellowed from a hundred throats.

Then a discreet hush as a respectable citizen came along — a lawyer named Porter Plumb who'd once been district attorney.

Charley Barrow waited till Plumb was out of hearing. Then he was at it again.

"Listen, men! When our cause is just we don't need to be squeamish. As the poet said —

128

'Lament who will
The mitre trampled low,
All are not murderers who kill;
The cause commends the blow.' "

Not many of them recognized it as a classic apology for lynching. But they roared approval. Barrow pressed his point, waving his arms, pouring out scholarly eloquence from the tip of his brandy-oiled tongue.

Every condition favored him. Sheriff Hooper was off with the militia, fighting Indians. His top deputies, reinforced by many of McEvoy's town police, were out scouring the hills for the Dillons and Major Norman.

"I ask you again, men! Shall we stand for it?"

Again a chorus of noes. A shrill voice called from the crowd. "I seen him duck into Miranda's place, Charley. He's hidin' there right now."

"Then what are we waiting for?"

Two hundred inflamed men surged up Galena toward Durant, the remittance man at their head. As they passed a saloon hitchrack one of them snatched a coiled lariat from a cowboy's saddle. "That's the stuff, Jake! Hoist him high!"

Jake, himself out of jail less than a week, bulled his way to the head of the mob and joined Barrow. "What about the bell tower, Charley?"

A tower with the town's fire bell loomed half a block to the right. It was fifty feet high and would make a perfect scaffold.

"Too close to the courthouse," Barrow decided. "We'll use that mine tipple at the top of Spring Street."

The mob swung east on Durant and went rumbling up the Row, parlor houses on one side and cribs on the other. Frightened women peered out and then jerked down the blinds. Dance music stopped in mid-note.

On rushed the crowd like a herd of maddened buffalo. It crossed Hunter Street. A block further, at Spring, the Row petered out. Barrow stopped them in front of a frame rooming house only a stone's throw north of the Midland Railroad's half finished depot.

The house was dark on both floors. It was a cheap place, but decent. Generally Miranda rented her rooms to hard working laborers.

Barrow appointed a committee of three. "You and you and you," he directed, "go in and fetch him out."

Three darted into the house. The others milled about in the street, waiting. A light came on upstairs. They heard a shrill protest from Miranda — "*No se puede . . .*"

"You just think we can't!" The jeer came from Jake, the man with the rope.

Out came the committee, dragging Alf Jenner. Panic paralyzed Jenner, dissolving his screams into thin sobs.

"Fetch him along," Barrow shouted. "This way." The ore tipple was a few hundred yards south, at the base of Aspen Mountain.

"Somebody's comin', Charley."

A man on a chestnut horse, leading an unsaddled calico, came loping up Spring Street. He reined to a stop beside Barrow. Wheeling, he faced the mob.

The surprise of it brought a sudden quiet. The mounted man didn't need to shout. "Listen, you fellas.

130

Use your heads and you'll see two good reasons for not stringin' him up. Want to hear 'em?"

The silence held a minute longer. Then a voice called from the dark. "Who is it? The law?"

"Not the law, Hank. It's that kid stage driver who gunned it out with Lockwood."

"Scoot him outa the way," Hank growled, "and let's get along with it."

But some wanted to listen. Only two weeks ago Wesley Brian had been the town's hero, a toast at every bar in Aspen. It wasn't every day that a hospital patient shot it out with a sneak killer.

"Talk fast, kid. We ain't got too much time."

"First reason's Major Norman," Wes explained. "Maybe the Dillons are holding him alive. They could figure him as a chip to trade with. But suppose you hang Jenner! What then? When Gil and Fred Dillon hear about it they put a slug through Norman."

It was solid logic and some of them saw it at once.

"What's yer other reason, kid?"

"This." A forty-five appeared in Wes Brian's hand. He aimed it at the committee of three, shocking them into looser holds on Jenner. "If anyone thinks it's not enough, speak up. Beat it, Jenner."

Alf Jenner twisted free. He darted between Miranda's house and a lumber pile. The night swallowed him and no one gave chase. Wes Brian's gun held the crowd sullenly in its tracks.

All but two. The two came at Wes, one from either side. "Get him, Charley." Jake dived for Brian's leg to pull him from the saddle.

Wes, expecting it, stood in his stirrups and brought the gun down on Jake's head. The sensitive thoroughbred reared as Wes wheeled him sharply against Barrow. A forehoof struck Barrow flush on the chin and sent him sprawling.

"What's goin' on?"

"Need any help, Brian?"

Two law officers appeared from the gloom of Spring Street and took stands beside Wes. "We heard a ruckus up this way," one panted, "and came arunnin'. Are we too late?"

"You're right on time, Grogan." Wes recognized them as Patrolmen Grogan and Thatcher.

Grogan drew his gun and took over. "Clear the street, you tinhorns. On the double."

Leaderless, the mob broke away, scattering toward the Cooper Avenue bars.

"I better run these two in," Thatcher growled. He slapped Jake and Barrow to consciousness, then marched them toward the city jail.

It left Wes alone with Grogan. Grogan put away his gun. "By mornin'," he predicted, "they'll cool off. Then Jenner can high-tail outa town."

"Which is another reason why I horned in," Wes said as he licked a cigaret. "Maybe it'll help to find the Dillons."

Grogan cocked an eye. "Yeh? How do you figure it?"

"Gil and Fred are hiding in the hills. Likely Jenner knows where they are. They're the only friends he's got. So if he can he'll join 'em."

132

Grogan mulled it over. "Humph! Maybe you got somethin'. The Dillons called at Jenner's cell the afternoon before they grabbed Norman. Likely they tipped Jenner where to find them."

"Here's the idea, Grogan. Round up twelve volunteers you can trust. Make six teams of two each. Only about six roads out of town. Let two men watch each. If Jenner sneaks by, let one man follow while the other reports to the courthouse."

"You're talkin', fella. Will do. Even if we lose Jenner it'll tip us to what direction we'd better look for the Dillons."

"And when you find the Dillons you'll find Roger Norman."

"Either dead or alive," Grogan nodded.

Wes rode to the Carson stage barn and put up his horses. From there he walked down Mill Street to the Clarendon. It was after midnight and only two people were in the lobby. A sleepy night clerk and a sleepless guest — Honora Norman.

"I heard shouting." Her tone was edged with dread. "Have they found . . . ?"

"Not a thing," Wes said quickly. He didn't need to ask why even at midnight she was here in the lobby, restless and distraught. Her face was dull and dead from the long weary watch. Waiting for a word about her father.

An immense pity filled Wes. "Look, Honora. I just rode forty miles and I feel kinda bushed. What about joinin' me for a cup of coffee?" He turned to Neal

Hutton, the night clerk. "Is it all right if we stoke up the kitchen stove?"

"Help yourself, Mr. Brian. The supper coals ought to still be hot." The clerk looked at the blanket roll on Wes's shoulder. "Meantime I'll book a room for you."

Wes dropped the roll on the floor. "Send this up, will you?"

A dim light burned in the deserted dining room and another hung in the kitchen. Wes and Honora went back there and found a cold pot of supper coffee. Wes stirred coals in the big range and added fuel.

While the coffee warmed he perched on the cook's stirring stool and Honora sat on a cane-bottom chair. "That ruckus you heard was just some drunks sounding off. Grogan chased 'em off to bed."

"You've ridden forty miles? Why?"

"I read about your Dad," he answered simply. "Thought I'd better pitch in and help find him."

Her stare was both mystified and grateful. "You came all the way here for that? But you hardly know him!"

"He's lost and needs finding." Wes let it go at that. "I got an idea. Listen." He explained his scheme for watching six roads out of Aspen.

The coffee boiled and he filled cups. They drank it black, not talking for a while, just sitting there in the Clarendon's dim, barny kitchen each with the same unspoken thought. Was there any real hope of finding Roger Norman alive? "You'll join one of the posses?" the girl asked presently.

"Maybe. Or maybe I'll just ride solo and play a few hunches. One is that the Dillons never did leave town.

134

Another is that they're holing up in the shaft-house of some worked-out mine."

"You've just come from your ranch? It's near Glenwood Springs, isn't it?"

"Yes, I put up some winter feed there. It's not really a ranch. Just a little hay farm. But it's a right pretty place." Glad to ease the tension Wes told her about his hay crop and his log cabin and his heifers. "I'd sure like to show 'em to you some time. Made a couple of good friends down that way." He told her about Colonel Clemson and Ray Plover.

What he didn't mention was a sniper's bullet fired at him barely thirteen hours ago. Neither did he mention the Ike Buford gang or tonight's tangle with a mob just three blocks east of this hotel.

"That's enough about me. What about you, Honora?"

She looked at him from tired, discouraged eyes. "I do nothing but wait, and worry — and wonder where he is. And hate myself for being out to a dance when it happened. It's driving me crazy. I ought to be doing something, Wesley. Like riding through the hills with the others . . ."

"Let me do the riding," Wes said gently.

"The only thing I'm sure of," the girl said firmly, "is that I'll stay right here in Aspen till they find him. No matter how long it takes." She sipped her coffee and then added, half irrelevantly: "I was offered a job today. At least it would keep me busy."

"A job? Where?"

"In Frank Bayard's office. He needs a secretary."

It's a wife he's after, Wes thought. The office job would keep her under Bayard's eye all the time. A smart operator, that fellow. The prospect annoyed Wes but he didn't let it show in his voice. "Yeh, I reckon Frank'll have lots of things to look after now that he's got himself a bonanza. By the way; it was Frank who got me that Cattle Creek quarter-section . . ."

He saw she wasn't listening. She was staring past him at a window. Her fixed gaze made him whirl about and for half a second Wes, too, saw a face pressed against the pane there. Then it was gone.

"Who was it?" Honora exclaimed nervously. "That man? I never saw him before. Did you?"

Wes crossed to the window, opened it, looked out into darkness. "Seems to me I saw him once, Honora. Maybe in a crowd at night. Or maybe he rode my stage one time. But I can't place him."

He leaned from the window to look both ways across the rear hitch lot. The racks were empty at this hour. At the lot's northeast corner, Mill and Cooper, a street lamp made a yellow dot. "Nobody in sight," Wes said.

The shot came just as he turned from the window and the sudden movement saved his life. The bullet zinged in and plunked against the kitchen's far wall. A rifle cracked from a poplar hedge along Monarch. As Wes jumped to one side a second bullet crashed glass from the pane.

"Better go to your room, Honora." Wes drew his forty-five and vaulted the sill.

136

He landed in the hitch lot and ran toward the hedge. From the dark beyond it he heard hoofbeats retreating down Monarch.

At the hedge he found nothing at all — except two empty rifle shells. They were 44–40s each with a UT factory mark on its cap end.

CHAPTER
FIFTEEN

In the morning Wes found Deputy Gavitt in the sheriff's office. "Has Jenner left town, Bob?"

Gavitt shook his head. "We're watchin' all six roads. Plus the ore trail up to Tourtelotte Park. Also the livery barns and outgoing stages."

"He might take off afoot," Wes thought, "straight through the brush."

"Maybe. But he wouldn't get far that way."

"Know anyone who uses this kind of ammunition?" Wes held up three empty UT rifle shells and explained where he'd picked them up.

Gavitt gave a low whistle. "Somebody around here don't like you, fella."

"He cut loose at me about noon yesterday, on Castle Creek. Thirteen hours and forty miles later he did it again right here in Aspen. We saw his face at the window. Seemed kinda familiar. But I can't pin it down."

The deputy asked a few questions and made notes. "I'll check the hardware stores and see if they stock UTs. You gonna join up with a posse?"

"I'll ride solo for a few days, Bob. I got a two-horse string and a posse couldn't keep up with me." Wes nodded toward a hitchrack where two mounts were tied, one saddled, the other with a light pack.

"Hold up your hand," Gavitt said, "and I'll swear you in. If you shoot it out with the Dillons it might as well be legal."

Wes rode out of town on the calico, leading the chestnut racer. A badge on his vest labeled him as an emergency deputy sheriff, like a score of other volunteers out scouring the hills. "We'll work Maroon Creek today, Patch."

A mile below town he turned up a cascading stream half the size of Roaring Fork itself. Its canyon was brushy, steep-walled, and in spots made swampy by beaver dams. A guard stepped out of an aspen thicket and hailed him. "You're wastin' your time, Brian. Alf Jenner hasn't passed by here."

"Unless he sneaked by you in the brush," Wes said. "I'll check as far as the lake, anyway."

It was ten miles to Maroon Lake and Wes made record time. Every five miles he changed his saddle from horse to horse. Rising sheer from the lake a row of fourteen thousand foot peaks marked the Elk Range. Maroon Pass notched through them, and over it innumerable jack trains had passed, freighting ore to a narrow gauge railhead in Gunnison County.

But today the road was deserted. Men working a shaft above the lake told Wes why. "A rock slide just this side of the pass. Take two months to clear a trail through it and by that time they figger to have rails into Aspen. So they're pilin' the ore up and waitin'."

"Seen any strangers out this way? Any camp smoke?"

"Not since the slide closed the trail. A few claims are being worked around here. All well known miners."

"Any hunters?"

"A few. But we know 'em. I was out myself the other day, up Willow Creek. Lots of meat up that way." The man narrowed his eyes as he remembered something. "I wasn't the only one up there, either. Had a bead on a buck when somebody beat me to him."

"Up Willow Creek?"

"Yeh, 'bout two mile up. When the buck dropped I turned around and came back. No mines up there. Some deer hunter from town, likely."

It was a thin chance but Wes played it. Changing mounts again he rode back down Maroon Creek and stopped at the mouth of a smaller stream coming in from the west. Only a steep bridle trail led up it. No use punishing both horses, so Wes picketed the chestnut and rode the calico.

Halfway up, the trail's steepness made him walk and lead his mount. The climb winded him and twice he stopped to rest. A dense forest closed about him. And still the trail twisted upward, zigzagging higher and higher above the canyon's bed until Wes could no longer hear the cascades below.

But after two miles the trail flattened and he came out in a mountain park. Here was Willow Creek again, this time riffling gently through an open meadow.

At the far head of the meadow, smoke curled upward above the tree tops. Camp smoke. Probably deer hunters. Yet it might be the Dillons. Wes tied his horse, took his carbine and moved forward afoot.

Half a mile from the smoke he climbed to a bench for a better look. From here he made out a small log hut with a dirt roof. Some trappers had once wintered up here, coming out with a pack of mink and marten. This was September, too early for trapping.

Yet someone was using the place. The fire was on the ground outside and Wes watched for other sign of life.

Presently he saw a man come from the creek with a bucket of water. The man threw the water on the camp fire. A second man appeared in the doorway and beckoned him inside.

They were two stocky men half a mile away and partly screened by weeds and leaves. It wasn't likely that they were the Dillons. Yet this could be a prearranged meeting place where Jenner, after his acquittal, would join them. It was only six steep miles from Aspen. Jenner might walk it by night and keep off the trails.

Wes pumped a shell into his rifle chamber and moved forward. A hundred yards from the hut he brought the stock to his cheek and kept an aim on the door. There was one door and one paneless window.

At fifty yards he heard voices inside. The door was closed, so Wes shifted direction to approach the window. From this new angle he saw two saddles. They were draped over a windfall. The horses might be hobbled somewhere near.

Advancing quietly to the window Wes peered in. Two men were cutting venison into strips. Neither was Gil or Fred Dillon.

One looked familiar and in a moment Wes remembered him. He stood erect and called through the window, "Hello there, Griffin."

Jote Griffin and a companion looked up, surprised but not alarmed. "It's that kid stage driver," Griffin exclaimed. "Whatcha doin' up here, fella?"

"What are *you* doing up here?" Wes countered.

They came out and joined him. The second man, a leather-faced guide, gave Wes a cup of coffee. They sat on a windfall. "I'm celebratin' some good luck," Jote Griffin said. "After I get me a bull elk I'll head for the bright lights of Denver."

"What good luck?" Wes asked curiously.

"Look what I got in the mail." Griffin showed Wes a letter with a check pinned to it. The check was for twenty-five hundred dollars. The letter said,

I can only conclude that Lockwood robbed you and gave the money to me to redeem a check. Since I cannot accept stolen money, I return it herewith to you.

Sincerely,
Joshua B. Wilbur.

"I'd kissed it goodbye," Griffin grinned.

He hadn't seen any sign of the Dillons or Roger Norman. His guide was an old-timer who'd crossed the range in '79 and Wes asked him a simple question.

"Put yourself in the place of the Dillons and Jenner. What trail would you pick to get out of Gilpin County?"

The guide freshened his quid and gave thought. "I'd go out over Pearl Pass," he decided, "by way of Castle Creek and Ashcroft. More dodgin' room that way. Plenty of brush fer a party to keep outa sight in."

"Thanks." Wes left them and went back to his horse. Stepping into the saddle he followed the trail to the foot of Willow Creek and picked up his remount.

It was twilight when he rode into Aspen. He took a room at the Clarendon and changed shirts. He shaved carefully with the hope of joining Honora at supper.

But Wes got no farther than the dining room door. Through it he saw Honora with Frank Bayard. The man's expensively tailored suiting made Wes feel shabby. His bold blond face had never looked more engaging or handsome as his hand reached across the table to Honora's. Nothing brash about it; just the right blend of sympathy and reassurance. Letting her know whom she could depend on in this anxious hour.

Wes backed away and took supper at the Delmonico. Waiting for his order he read today's *Times*. It said that Aspen's newest silver king, Frank Bayard, had just purchased a ten thousand acre cattle ranch on Grand River, below Glenwood Springs. The paper said it was a show place with a ten-room stone mansion. In midwinter Bayard could bask in comfort down there, when snows got too deep in Aspen.

And why not? The *Lost Friend* was now earning three thousand dollars per day. *And me with a dinky quarter-section! And him holding my note even for that!*

In the morning Wes Brian again rode out of town, leading a remount. He turned up Castle Creek toward Ashcroft. West Aspen Mountain rose to his left with its parks already turning yellow. The stream here was about the size of Maroon Creek and at the first ford a lookout stopped him. "You won't ketch Jenner up this way. He hasn't gone by."

"He hasn't gone by anywhere," Wes said.

He lingered through a cigaret and then jogged on. After a few miles he heard wheels rumbling toward him downcanyon. A stagecoach hove in sight with Chip Jackson driving. Chip had the short run. Aspen to Ashcroft. He drove up one day and back the next. It was only thirteen miles.

"Hi, Wes." Chip pulled to a stop for a chat and to rest his horses. "Heard talk about you as I left town yesterday morning."

"Nothing bad, I hope." Wes hooked a leg around his saddle horn and handed up the makings.

"It was about a lynch party you stopped, at midnight. I had to pull out before I got the lowdown on it. Where did it happen?"

"Right in front of Miranda's roomin' house," Wes said. "By the way, you haven't seen that bird Jenner, have you?"

"Not hide nor hair of him. And don't ask me about the Dillons. People have stopped me 'steen times to ask about 'em. Take care of yourself, Wes." Chip gathered his reins to drive on when a thought jolted him. He sat the brake and sat there with his mouth hanging open.

"Did you say Miranda?" he blurted suddenly.

144

"Sure I did. They dragged Jenner out of her house and . . ."

"Miranda!" Chip popped a gloved hand on his knee. His eyes rounded. "Either it's a coincidence or I've been suckered. And you too, Wes."

"What about Miranda? Let's have it, Chip."

"Just as I was ready to pull out of Aspen at daybreak yesterday, Miranda showed up with her aunt. She bought her aunt a one-way fare to Highland and put her on the stage. She said her aunt didn't savvy any English. Some mine near Highland, she said, had hired her aunt as a cook. The mine people would meet her if I'd be good enough to put her off there."

"And did you put her off there?"

"Sure. Why not?"

"Did anyone meet her?"

"I didn't notice. Had to drive right on. They's a dozen mines around there with crews big enough to need a cook. Where you goin', Wes?"

Wes had heard enough. Leading his mount, he was off at a trot up the Castle Creek trail.

Highland, halfway between Aspen and Ashcroft, was already a ghost town. A few optimists had started a settlement there back in '81, but in a year or so they'd scattered either upcreek to Ashcroft or downcreek to Aspen. Nothing remained except a half dozen empty, tumbledown shacks.

No life was in sight when Wes got to them. From upmountain to the left came the chug of a hoist engine. The *Little Annie*, a good producing mine, was up there. Bigger and better properties, like the *Eclipse* and the *Climax*, lay beyond, high on the ridge, but their outlet to Aspen was north through Tourtelotte Park. Wes couldn't believe that any one of them would hire a cook and tell her to get off the stage at Highland.

From the opposite direction, Conundrum Creek came plunging down a gorge to meet Castle Creek here. A tortured road led up it, a trail of bleak wilderness, steep, thorn-locked, treacherous, a land of narrow footings slanting toward Cathedral Peak and Triangle Pass. Dead Men's Gulch, people called Conundrum. In a March storm three years ago five men were buried under a snow slide up there. Wes himself had helped dig out the bodies.

Fugitives like the Dillons, hiding up that gulch, would be hard to find.

Wes made sure that no one was in the several shacks at Highland. As he looked into the last of them a huge owl came flapping out. Then Wes Brian quit the stage road, forded Castle Creek and dismounted where Conundrum came into it.

He pushed a little way up the smaller stream through a tangle of wild cherry. *If I had a bundle to get rid of, where would I hide it?*

Wes lay flat to reach into a badger hole. He raked under a brush pile and peered under an overhanging bank. Further on he came to a hollow, rotting log.

He kneeled at one end to look in. There it was! The bundle. The thing a man would need to get rid of, to travel afoot through the bush.

146

From the hollow log Wes pulled out a woman's skirt and blouse and *reboza*. Also a black shawl and a wig of gray hair. Miranda's aunt!

Footprints in the sand led up the creek bank and only Jenner could have made them. Jenner outfitted by Miranda to fool a sleepy stage driver at dim dawn. Once in the brush, Jenner would get shed of these duds and hurry on to meet the Dillons.

The man was a day ahead of Wes. But afoot he couldn't travel fast. And every step of the way he'd need to keep out of sight in the brush. Wes kneeled to look closely at a footprint by the water's edge. Not the print of a riding boot. This was the print of a square-toed shoe with a broad heel.

A horse couldn't be ridden or led through this creek-bank thicket. But a wagon trail led up Conundrum; Wes had traveled it, knew that it crossed and recrossed the creek every half mile or so. He went back to his horses, mounted one and led the other.

The trail up Conundrum was an ore road once in heavy use by silver properties in the gulch. Five years ago the St. Elmo, just above here, had worked full shifts. A year later the Cummings lode had changed hands for twenty thousand dollars. But the play this way had been short-lived. Richer claims on Aspen and Smuggler Mountains, and up around Ashcroft, had taken the limelight. Most of the gulch diggings were shut down. At Carey's Camp, scene of the great avalanche disaster three winters ago, there wasn't even a caretaker.

Sign on the ore trail told Wes that a mounted posse had already worked this gulch. Lookouts might be watching even now from high points on the mountain. Knowing that, Jenner would keep to the brush.

Which would slow him to a crawl. Wes, riding fast up an open trail, would gain on him with every stride.

When the trail crossed the creek he looked again for shoe-prints. There they were — square toes and broad heels. Jenner was hugging water all the way. Part of the time he'd wade riffles. But generally the fall was too torrential for that; it would keep him ashore fighting his way through thorny thickets.

Wes himself kept on the trail. In half a mile it again forded the creek and again he saw Jenner's sign in the sand. *I don't envy him, Patch.* The man would be scratched ragged after a few miles of this.

Wes changed his saddle from Patch to Prince. Pressing on up the trail he occasionally saw tailings from a shaft. And a scattering of cabins. In one cabin he found a caretaker. Near another a two-man shift was at work, one man mucking below and the other above at a windlass.

Neither the caretaker nor the windlass man had seen Jenner pass. Nor the Dillon brothers. "A sheriff's outfit rid by here day before yesterday, lookin' fer Norman."

"Alf Jenner sneaked by you in the brush yesterday," Wes told them.

He pushed on, crossing and recrossing the creek. At each crossing he made sure that Jenner was still ahead of him.

Seven miles up Conundrum he sighted Carey's Camp. Its tailing dumps made gray splashes against the gold of the hillside aspens. The three brown dots were cabins which Wes remembered only too well.

To his surprise, the shoe-prints of Jenner left the creek and headed straight toward the three cabins. Wes dismounted, carbine in hand. He moved forward afoot. A hundred yards from camp he stopped again, alert for any sign of life there.

CHAPTER
SIXTEEN

Was it the end of the chase? This deserted camp was a likely place for the Dillons to wait for Jenner. No horses were in sight. No saddles. But if Jenner had joined them late yesterday they'd be gone by now. Gone asaddle, upgulch toward Triangle Pass. Or at the near base of Cathedral Peak they might strike for the head of Piney Creek and follow it down to Ashcroft. From Ashcroft they could make it over Pearl Pass to the Gunnison country.

Wes waited for wary minutes, watching the cabins. The nearest and biggest one, he remembered, had been Jimmie Thorne's. If Gil and Fred Dillon were there they'd have him covered. Maybe from one of the shacks, maybe from the nearby aspens. The cabins looked as still and ghostly as on that bleak April morning, three years ago, when Wes had arrived here with Johnny Steele's rescue party. It was five weeks after a snow slide had buried the camp thirty feet deep.

All they'd dug out was five frozen bodies. And how plain the sign! The five still at a card table. An alarm clock with the hands stopped at 7.57, the exact time of the avalanche; the alarm set for six in the morning. Wes remembered thawing the clock out — his shock when the hands got to six and the alarm actually went off, five weeks late!

But most of all he remembered Bruiser. No one in Aspen would ever forget Bruiser. A faint noise had made them look under a bunk — and there lay Thorne's pet bulldog, skin and bones after five starvation weeks. They'd taken Bruiser to Aspen, nursed him to health. And the little dog had made the headlines from coast to coast. Aspen folks had put a solid silver collar on him and shipped him to Thorne's sister in New York.

A shrine of courage, this camp. To it now had come the skulking coward, Jenner. The insolence of it angered Wes Brian as he whipped his rifle level. Eyes alert, he advanced toward the nearest cabin.

No one challenged him. The door hung askew on one hinge. Wes looked into an empty room. Scampering pack mice made the only sound.

It was the same at the other two cabins. One had a stove with fresh-broken fuel by it. Whoever had last stopped here didn't have an axe. The bunks had no blankets; but fresh pine twigs on one meant that it had been slept on last night.

Wes circled the camp and found no horse sign. What shoe sign he found was Jenner's. Jenner had arrived alone; he'd left alone.

It must have been dark when the man got here, Wes reasoned. Afoot and fighting brush, it would take Jenner all day to come seven miles up Conundrum. Arriving after nightfall he'd be afraid to go on in the dark. And dead tired. So he'd stopped for the night. At daybreak he'd move on to meet the Dillons.

Now it was noon, so the man's start was only six hours. Wes went to his horses and rode on upgulch, keeping to the trail.

Above Carey's Camp the gulch steepened. In spots it narrowed to a box gorge with staircase waterfalls plunging through, forcing the trail to a high, mountainside ledge. Jenner couldn't have gone through the gorge. For a while Wes lost all sign of him.

A band of wild sheep leaped across the ledge and raced up a niche in the cliff.

Then the trail dipped to meet the creek again, striking it in a heaver dam meadow snug against the toe of Cathedral Peak. In marshy ground there Wes again picked up the square-toed shoe-prints. He followed them to a split in the trail.

One fork led straight ahead toward Triangle Pass. A pass fit only for goats. The other fork turned at right angles east. Wes knew that it led to the head of Piney Creek and down the Piney to Ashcroft.

Square-toes had turned east toward the Piney.

Wes changed horses and rode that way at a trot. His speed since noon had more than doubled Jenner's and the man couldn't be very far ahead.

The trail led upward toward a timbered saddle. Electric Pass, some called it, dividing the watershed of Conundrum from the watershed of Piney. Cathedral Peak reared high on the right with Hayden Peak on the left. Between lay a plateau of fir forest, the trail threading through tall, close-spaced trees.

The trees were slim spires, their tiny-needled branches slanting downward like the skirts of glossy green gowns. Abruptly they opened into a small, circular swale.

A parklike swale with high grass, and in it Wes saw three saddled horses. Two men squatted by a smokeless fire. One fanned the blaze with his hat while the other stripped bacon into a pan. A third man lay on his back, hat over his eyes, sleeping.

The two at the fire saw Wes at the moment he saw them. One snatched a rifle and fired. The other ran to the horses. The chestnut reared as Wes jumped from the saddle. He had his carbine in hand and he hit the ground shooting. The forest shadowed him and made Fred Dillon miss.

Fred, on his feet now, fired again. "Get him, Gil!"

But it was Jenner and not Gil who nearly got Wes Brian. Jenner was up and shooting. The others had armed him with a holster gun. He emptied it at Wes while Wes was still shooting it out with Fred Dillon.

Fred buckled to his knees, triggering wildly and cursing his brother Gil. Hoofbeats told on Gil. Gil had jumped to a saddle and was pounding off through the woods.

Jenner's third bullet drew blood from Wes. Wes dodged behind a twin fir and fired twice through the split, once at Fred, once at Jenner. Fred fell forward on his rifle. Jenner, ragged and hairy, ran toward a horse and was nearly there when he stumbled. He crawled a little way, tried to pull himself up by a stirrup. Then he went flat on his face, silent and motionless.

153

A sting at his cheek made Wes swab his sleeve over it. The sleeve came away bloody. He reloaded his carbine and advanced to Fred Dillon. He rolled the man face up. "What did you do with Norman? Where is he?"

Fred Dillon didn't and couldn't answer. He was dead.

Jenner wasn't. His chest was shot clean through but he had life left. One breath was all Wes needed.

"What did they do with him?" he demanded. "Major Norman?"

Glassy eyes stared at him. Jenner's lips moved but said nothing. Maybe he knew and maybe he didn't.

Wes Brian had two choices. He could chase Gil Dillon. Or he could try to coax an answer from Jenner. He couldn't do both. Nor would Jenner last long.

"Look. I'm the guy kept 'em from lynching you down at Aspen. You got nothing to lose. What did they do with Norman?"

Again the lips moved. This time a faint word came. "Water."

One of the Dillon horses had a canteen on it. Wes gave Jenner a few swallows. "Is he alive somewhere? Or did they drop him down a shaft?"

Jenner didn't curse him. He didn't even look hostile. He lay there in his brush-torn rags like a man too weary for talk and too hopeless to care.

Wes kept at it, coaxing, fretting impatiently. Every minute Gil was getting further away.

The sun was down and twilight dimmed the forest. Darkness would mean a twelve hour start for Gil. He could be across the range by morning.

Yet as long as Jenner had a breath of life Wes couldn't leave him. A word from the man might unlock the mystery of Roger Norman. The main goal was to find Norman.

Dark came with its high altitude chill. Again Jenner's lips gave up two syllables. "Whisky." Wes had none of his own. But the Dillons had unrolled a light pack and Wes found a pint in it. Jenner seemed grateful as the liquor slid down his throat.

He lived an hour after nightfall and with his last breath he answered Wes. "I don't know," Alf Jenner said. A minute later he was dead.

Wes built a fire and fed himself. His first urge was to press on through the night and report to the law at Ashcroft. Yet something impelled him not to leave this spot till he'd searched all around it for Norman.

Here he'd found the Dillons. So here, dead or alive, he might also find their prisoner. In any case he must look into every shaft and test pit between here and the Piney. If they'd murdered Norman near here, dropping him into a pit would be a quick way to hide the crime.

The tarp of the Dillon pack was wide enough to wrap two bodies. When it was done Wes hobbled all four horses. The bullet cut on his cheek wasn't deep and he covered it with a sliver of tape. A moon climbed over the forest and gave mellow light to his sleep.

After a dawn breakfast he circled the camp looking for a mound of earth, a test hole, a brush pile. A fruitless search made him conclude they hadn't buried a victim at or near this spot.

He loaded the tarp-wrapped bodies on the Dillon horses and saddled Prince. Patch came along without being led. From here on the trail was wooded but gave fair footing. Presently it wound downward to the headwaters of Piney.

A prospector's diggings halted Wes. He made a torch of dead pine needles and dropped it into the hole. A brief glare at the bottom showed nothing. Wes mounted and rode on.

A small fork of Piney riffled by the trail. High to the right loomed the snowy crags of Castle and Pearl Mountains. Here the path was a twisting lane through parks of aspen. Again Wes came to a test pit and again he dropped a flare into it.

Further on he came to a shaft so deep that a dropped torch took three watch-ticks before sizzling out in water at the bottom. There were many such deserted shafts in the hills and any one of them could hide Roger Norman.

The bleak thought discouraged Wes as he rode on. The country opened a little. A turquoise mirror below him was Cathedral Lake. Just south of it lay Senator Tabor's famed *Montezuma* mine. From it a fortune in ore had been wheeled over Pearl Pass to a railhead at Crested Butte.

Wes turned another twist of the trail and saw a pile of gray tailings. It was a small pile, so the test hole wasn't very deep. A pick, shovel and bar on the brim of it made it look like a man was still at work there. Nearby, at the edge of the woods, were two grazing mules.

156

Maybe this prospector could tell him something. Wes rode to the test hole and dismounted. No sound of digging came from it.

He peered down into a hole only about five feet deep. A doubled-up shape lay at the bottom. In a moment Wes knew it was a man, either dead or helpless.

He ran to a horse and took a rope from its pack. After tying the rope to a rock he dropped the other end into the hole. He lowered himself down there and struck a match. A stench, and the cold stiffness of the body, meant that this man had been dead for days.

Wes Brian's first thought was Norman. But the flare of his second match assured him it wasn't Norman. A prospector, no doubt. A charge of his own dynamite, or even the explosion of a cap could have left him helpless down here.

Wes secured the rope around him, then clambered from the pit. Bracing himself he pulled the weight up, brought it over the rim into sunlight.

The man's head was ghastly. A bullet drilled through it must have brought instant death. Wes's quick guess was that he'd been shot while standing at the rim of the pit and had toppled into it. For there were no tools below.

The victim himself wasn't armed. He was a rugged type, dressed in miner's boots and corduroys. Wes had never seen him before. The hip pocket wallet might identify him. Wes looked through it and found money — three hundred sixty dollars in bills. So the motive wasn't robbery.

Then he found a lodge card made out to John Hostetter.

Hostetter! The name startled Wes. That mystery letter from Ashcroft! About the soft roof of a stope. Wes had never been able to make sense out of it. The one clear thing about it was the signature. J. Hostetter.

Here lay J. Hostetter! Shot by a rifleman, most likely. A pistol-armed killer couldn't get close enough without being seen. The nearest cover was an aspen copse about a hundred yards away.

Hostetter's camp was probably in those aspens. An enemy creeping up on him there might see him getting ready for work at the test pit. One rifle shot from the aspens would be enough.

Wes walked grimly over there for a look. He found a pack and a grubstake and a fly of canvas. The typical rude camp of a prospector. The packaging of the grubstake showed that it had been bought at the Louis Tauscher store at Ashcroft.

Wes moved along the edge of the trees to the spot nearest the test pit. Here was the likely place for the sniper to shoot from. On the ground lay an empty brass shell. The shell was from a 44–40 rifle.

Wes looked at the cap end of it, compared it with three other empty shells in his pocket. This one, like the others, was a UT.

CHAPTER
SEVENTEEN

Trailing into Castle Street with three dead men, Wes Brian made a sensation. All of Ashcroft crowded around as he told his story and delivered his cargo to the constable.

"Gosh! Looks like you rounded up everybody but Norman!"

"That's Hostetter, all right. Criminy! Who do you reckon had it in fer him?"

"You say one of them Dillon buggers got away? Which way did he go?"

The town looked jaded and shrunk, Wes thought, compared with his last visit here. A few years ago Ashcroft had had four hotels and now there was only one. While Aspen grew and boomed, Ashcroft, once called "The Mining Wonder of the West," was already fading. Railroads would come to Aspen but none would come here, where altitude made the town a snowbound wilderness six months in every year.

Wes turned the Dillon horses over to the constable and put up his own at Tauscher's barn. Then he crossed to the drugstore. "Is Doctor Eyssell in?" Wes touched the blood-stained strip of tape at his cheek.

"Hugo Eyssell sold out and moved to Kansas City," the druggist told him. "I'll fix you up myself, son."

While the man cleaned the cut and put on a fresh dressing, Wes showed him four empty rifle shells. "Anybody in town ever sell this brand of cartridge?"

"UTs? Sure. Louie Tauscher carries 'em. Bought a box myself, last time I went deer huntin'."

"Did you know a miner named Hostetter?"

"No. But I've heard plenty. There was a good deal of talk about him, week or so back."

"Yeh? Why?"

"He came through here on his way to Telluride. Stopped at Gus Gleason's bar and Gus made a deal with him. It's a habit Gus has. We call him the Grubstaker."

"So Hostetter went up Piney with a mule-load of grub?"

The druggist nodded. "And next day we got news from Aspen. Seems Hostetter sold his claim down there too soon. He thought it was a bust, but it wasn't. There you are, son."

With a clean patch on his cheek, Wes went over to Tauscher's store. The store also held the post office. Yes, Wes was told there, UT ammunition was carried in stock and had been for years. Any man in Ashcroft, or any stranger passing through, could have bought UT shells at Tauscher's.

Ashcroft still had three saloons and the least respectable of them was Gleason's. Wes found a one-eyed bartender serving a couple of freighters. A faro bank at the back had no trade at the moment.

"Gleason in?" Wes asked.

"Not today. Gus went to Aspen on business. Anything you want to know?"

"He grubstaked a man named Hostetter?"

"He sure did. Right here at this bar. The regular deal. I witnessed it myself. I've seen Gus make a dozen like it. All the grub and powder a guy needs fer sixty days, in exchange for a third of what he strikes worth filin' on."

"Did Hostetter quarrel with anyone, while he was here?"

"Nope. He didn't have time to. Wasn't in town only long enough to make that grubstake deal and load his mules."

One of the freighters spoke up. "I knew Hostetter well. He wasn't the quarrelin' kind. Kept his mouth shut, generally. A right peaceable fella."

Wes asked at the other saloons without learning anything new. Night came and he took a room at the Covert House. He'd have to let others beat the hills for Gil Dillon. For early tomorrow Wes himself must ride down to Aspen, the county seat. He'd be needed at the inquests over John Hostetter, Alf Jenner and Fred Dillon.

The Dillon case was fairly clear. There was no reason to connect it with Hostetter. The Dillons and Hostetter apparently had nothing in common.

But Hostetter and Wesley Brian *did* have something in common — an empty UT shell. Each had been fired at by a sniper using UTs. Why?

161

Wes fell asleep, puzzling over it. According to the Covert House registry book, this was the very room John Hostetter had slept in on his overnight stop at Ashcroft.

In the morning Wes saddled Patch. Leading Prince, he headed down the stage road to Aspen.

The Aspen Block, pressed brick trimmed with cut stone, was the town's newest and finest building. The First National Bank occupied the lower floor while directly above, with corner windows giving to both Hyman and Galena Streets, were the quarters of Aspen's most popular and prosperous broker.

After fitting the suite with deep carpets and handsome mahogany furniture, Frank Bayard had moved in only yesterday. There was an elegant outer office where his secretary would receive clients. The secretary's desk was unoccupied as yet, for Honora Norman hadn't accepted the job. But Bayard felt quite certain she would. For one thing she'd be needing money. But most of all she'd want to be where news about her father would be likely to come even before it reached the courthouse. Frank Bayard had seen to that by posting a five thousand dollar reward for information leading to the finding of Roger Norman.

He could easily afford it. Money was rolling in faster than it could be spent or invested. Already the reward had paid a rich dividend in gratitude from the lost man's daughter.

Swinging a cane and with a carnation in his buttonhole, Frank Bayard went briskly up the steps and opened his office door. The smartness of this setting brought a cocksure smile to his face. Everything about it spelled success. It was just the frame he needed to impress Honora.

He crossed to the door of his private office. When he entered it the smile left his face. Gus Gleason sat there, hat on, feet on the table, befouling the office with stogie smoke. "Come in, pardner," the man invited impudently, "and make yourself at home."

"Get out!" A pitch of anger shrilled Bayard's voice. "You know better than to come here."

Gleason grinned amiably. "Sure, pardner. We're to meet at the Abbey bar if anything comes up. We just happen to stand elbow to elbow at the deep end. You said you'd drop in there for a quick one at noon every day."

"Well?"

"I was there yesterday and you didn't show up. So here I am, pardner."

"What do you want? And stop calling me pardner."

"A little expense money," Gleason said. "Ten thousand'll do."

Bayard was expecting it and had a ready answer. "You haven't earned it yet."

"I've half earned it."

"Half is as good as nothing. The half that's left can still blow us to hell."

Gleason puffed his stogie, nodding. "You mean Brian." His mouth twisted and his voice took a lower tone. "Don't worry about *him*. I made two tries and the next time I won't miss. Top of all that they's other

163

parties that figure to beat me to him. Ran onto 'em at a bar. That proddy Buford bunch that's been raisin' hob down at Fryin' Pan."

"Ike Buford? Where does he come in?"

Gleason shrugged. "All I know is he's on the prod after Brian. Him and his outfit figure to burn Brian down, soon as Ike gets his arm out of a sling."

"I don't care who burns him down, just so it happens. Until it does you don't get a red cent. Is that clear?"

The Ashcroft man eyed the broker curiously. At their last meeting Bayard hadn't dared defy him like this. "You're crackin' a whip, fella. Let's have it. Whatta you got?"

Bayard moved closer and lowered his voice. "Just this. You killed Hostetter. With a UT shell. Then when you tried to kill Brian with a shell out of the same box, a witness saw your face at the window. The face was strange to her. But she'll know it if she ever sees it again."

Gleason's eyes narrowed. "So she saw me, huh?"

A calculation in the slitted eyes sent a chill through Bayard, made him sorry he'd spoken. It came to him for the first time how brutally ruthless this man was. For money he was out to kill two men. To save his neck he'd hardly hesitate to kill a witness.

"Okay, pardner. I'll keep out of her way." But the calculating gleam was still there. "No chance of her seein' me up here. So let's talk business."

"There's every chance," Bayard warned him, "of her seeing you up here. I've offered her a job in the office.

164

She may decide to take it any minute. Even if she doesn't she'll be coming up here to see if a reward I posted has brought results."

"In that case I better be goin'." Gus Gleason got up and slouched toward the door.

With his hand on the knob he turned and a cold deadliness replaced his impudent smirk. "Get this, Bayard. Soon as Brian's taken care of I want a fast, full pay-off. Try to wiggle out of it and your funeral'll happen right after Brian's."

He puffed his stogie to a glow and then dropped it on the rug.

As the clink of the man's spurs died away Bayard picked up the smoke, opened a window and threw it to the street. He knew with a chilling sureness that Gleason wasn't bluffing. Having killed Hostetter, he had nothing to lose by killing again. First Brian. Then anyone who could identify him as a killer. Like a girl who, past midnight in the Clarendon kitchen, had seen his face at a window. Or like Frank Bayard who if exposed in fraud might break down and tell tales.

If I pay him off, he'll kill me to shut my mouth!

Fingers of fear touched Bayard. What good would a million dollars be if Gleason came after him with a gun?

For a long time Bayard sweated out the question — and could find only one answer. He must hire a bodyguard. A man even quicker with a gun than Gus Gleason. The guard need know nothing at all except that Gleason was a threat.

CHAPTER
EIGHTEEN

The inquests at Aspen held Wes three days. The first was a joint inquest over Alf Jenner and Fred Dillon. Wes was the main witness. The deceased met death, the jury decided promptly, while resisting arrest by a sworn deputy of the law.

"The only kick we got," one juryman said, "is that you let Gil get away."

The second inquest, over the body of John Hostetter, took longer. A crowd of the curious jammed the inquiry room and among them was Harv Random. "I'm still scratching my noggin," the engineer said to Wes Brian, "over that letter he sent you. The stope roof was soft, all right. I shored it up. But why the heck did he write *you* about it?"

The coroner selected his jury and the last man he beckoned was Harv Random. A grubstake agreement was offered in evidence. It was signed by John Hostetter and Gus Gleason, and witnessed by Gleason's bartender. Mr. Covert of the Covert House told about Hostetter arriving after dark, staying all night, then early in the morning heading up Piney Creek to prospect for sixty days.

Then Wes Brian told about finding the body. He showed an empty UT shell. The contents of the dead man's pockets were spread out for the jury's inspection.

"Murder by an unknown rifleman," the jury decreed.

Wes hurried away to find Honora. She wasn't at the hotel. Later he saw her walking north on Galena.

Before he could catch up she turned into the stairway entrance of the new Aspen Block. As Wes got to the second floor she was disappearing into an office.

The name on the frosted glass was Frank Bayard.

A man came along the hall and delayed Wes a minute. "Want to double that bet, Wes? A mile of track a day, the Midland's laying."

"No thanks, Dave," Wes said absently. He'd almost forgotten a ten dollar bet he'd made more than two months ago.

When he went in Honora was seating herself at a secretary's desk. She greeted him with mock formality. "Good morning, sir. May I sell you some stocks? We're quoting *Bob Ingersoll* at par. And if you like . . ."

His look stopped her and brought a mist to her eyes. "You wonder how I can chatter this way. With my father not found yet! I'm just singing in the dark, Wesley. Anything to get my mind off of it. Have you heard about the reward?"

He nodded. The *Times* had been full of it. A cash reward posted by Frank Bayard at the bank. "That's one reason I came in." Wes took off his hat but didn't sit down. "I'm joining the search again. I'd hate for you to think I'm after a reward. I'm hunting him for *you*, Honora."

Her face softened. "You're so good to me, both of you! Frank for offering the reward and you for riding the hills day and night!"

"The reward will help," Wes admitted. "It'll put a thousand eyes to work."

"And they'll come straight here," Honora said, "if they see anything. That's really what made me take the job. To be on hand if . . ." An anxious pleading crept into her voice. "Do you really think there's any hope?"

He wanted to comfort her, so Wes gave her the only thin ray of hope which had occurred to him. "Kinda funny the Dillons made Jenner walk that far. They could've met him closer in. Say at Carey's Camp where he stayed all night."

Her puzzled look made him explain further. "Let's say he expected to meet them at Carey's Camp. But when he got there the place was empty. He stayed all night and the next day hiked on upcreek. Found 'em somewhere near Electric Pass and they camped smack on the trail there. Why?"

"Yes? Why?" Honora prompted eagerly.

"I don't know. But let's take a long shot guess. Suppose Major Norman got away from 'em and took off upcreek through the brush. They'd chase him. Maybe that's why Jenner didn't find 'em at Carey's Camp. Maybe they were beating the bush for Major Norman. If they couldn't find him, what would they do?"

"What *would* they do, Wesley?"

"He was somewhere at the head of Conundrum. Only two ways he could get out. The hard way, Triangle

168

Pass, which only a goat can climb. Or that flat, easy saddle they call Electric Pass, leading straight toward Ashcroft. They might figure he'd pick the easy way — and lay for him."

"Oh!" A desperate hope flickered in the blue eyes. "Instead, it was *you* who came along!"

"Don't pin any bets on it," Wes warned. "Forty men are searching the timber at the top of Conundrum. I'm heading that way myself."

"Stay with the others," she begged. "You need more than two eyes. I'm afraid for you, Wesley." She remembered he'd been shot at twice — and by someone other than the Dillons.

He looked curiously about the plush office. "Is your boss in?"

"Mr. Random took him up to the mine," Honora said, "to show him a new rich vein of galena. They're putting on more men to increase production."

"And what do *you* do? Make out the payroll?"

A bland voice answered from the doorway. "That and lots more, Wes. She keeps track of my appointments and charms my clients." Frank Bayard loomed there, big and blond and fastidiously groomed, a sharp contrast to Wes Brian's weathered ruggedness. Bayard with a cane, Wes with a gun at his hip and bullet holes through his hat. Bayard with a wing collar and Wes collarless, his flannel shirt open at the throat. "She'll keep an eye on that promissory note of yours, cowboy, and dun you if you don't pony up the interest."

Wes left in a mood of depression. He didn't analyze it till he was saddling Patch at the stable. *You're just*

169

feeling sorry for yourself, Wes Brian. What chance has a shoestring saddle man got with a silver king like Bayard?

He'd already sent Prince back to Colonel Clemson with a note of thanks. Now that no forced, deadline ride lay ahead, it wasn't fair to use the colonel's thoroughbred any longer. Wes tied a light pack back of the calico's saddle. Then he stopped at the courthouse to check with Gavitt.

"No use working that Conundrum country," Gavitt advised. "Everybody else is stumbling over each other there. Better pick one of these rumours and run it down." He thumbed toward a sheaf of reports.

Wes glanced through them. A man resembling Gil Dillon had been seen near Bowman, in Taylor Park. A brown horse resembling Gil's was seen running loose near the narrow gauge track below Crested Butte.

There were ten such rumours, all conflicting. One, sent in by a sheepherder, said a man of Gil's description had been seen near Marble, at the top of Rock Creek.

"Any of 'em could be true," Gavitt thought, "except the last one. To get to Marble from where you last saw him. Gil would need to cross the divide at Triangle Pass and then cross back into this county at Schofield Pass. He'd need wings for that."

Wes mulled it over. "He might think you'd think that way. Have you covered Marble?"

The acting sheriff shook his head. "No sense in it. He wouldn't cross the range twice."

"Then I'll cover it myself," Wes decided.

The crowflight distance to Marble was only twenty miles but by trail it was twice that far. Wes took two days for it, camping overnight at the base of Haystack Mountain. Late the second afternoon he struck Rock Creek at Lily Lake. A short ride upstream from there brought him to the quarries at Marble.

The place always amazed Wes. Carting silver ore across the range was one thing. But how could they afford to cart stone?

"Look, young fella," the storeman there said. "This here's the finest marble in the world. Lots of silver ore's worth less per pound. Anyway after next month we won't have to haul it over the hump any more. Not after the track gets to Satank."

The storeman hadn't seen anyone like Gil Dillon. Wes put up overnight and in the morning went hunting for a sheep-herder. Locating the herder took another two days. It was near sundown when a bleating lured Wes up a steep mountainside. The sheep were bedding down just under McClure Pass.

The herder was a Mexican. "Yes, señor, I have seen a man like that. He rides a brown horse and wears a black hat."

"Which way was he heading?"

"He fords Rock Creek where the stones are red. From there he rides the water that way." The herder pointed north.

"What time of day was it?"

"It is almost dark. Soon I find the place where he camp in the bushes all day."

Wes rode back down to the creek, easing his mount gently down the steepness. Rock Creek riffled due north, and in less than twenty miles it would meet Roaring Fork at Satank. Satank was a newborn grading camp much like Frying Pan City.

And only three miles north of Satank, by a ridge shortcut, was Wes Brian's own Cattle Creek cabin. *Which means, Patch old boy, that the guy's headin' straight toward home sweet home!*

Wes rode on downcreek. Presently the valley narrowed and became hemmed by red stone walls. Had Gil Dillon passed here four days ago? Lots of men wore black hats and rode brown horses.

But this one camped out of sight by day and rode by night. Gil Dillon would travel like that.

By this route he'd strike the line of construction camps along Roaring Fork, where two railroads were racing upstream to Aspen. Camps of nameless nondescripts, laborers imported in droves from Pueblo and Denver. Trains loaded with ties and bridge timbers ran to the end of rails and Gil might ride one of them back to Leadville or Denver. Or he might mix with the toughies of Satank or Glenwood Springs, brazening it out there.

Darkness blanketed the canyon as Wes jogged on down Rock Creek. An easy pace would take him through Satank and on to his Cattle Creek cabin by daybreak. He could rest there and then pick up the chase again. A few hours didn't matter, since the man on the brown horse had a four day start.

172

Gil Dillon, he reasoned, might easily take a chance on being picked up by the law. For unless Roger Norman was found dead, no murder charge could be placed against Gil. No body, no crime. At present he was wanted for questioning, and on "suspicion of kidnapping." But even that charge wouldn't stand up in court. The only case against Gil was that the Dillons had a motive for kidnapping Norman, and that they'd left Aspen on the night of Norman's disappearance.

Any smart lawyer could get him off. Still, Gil had to be run down. Wes jogged resolutely on through the dark, fording and refording the creek as its current swung from one red wall to another.

At the mouth of Avalanche Creek he unsaddled, rested Patch for an hour. It was after midnight when he rode on. Bright moonlight flooded the trail as the timber thinned, pine giving way to scrub oak and cottonwood. With each mile the valley widened.

Three miles below Avalanche Creek, hoof sounds alerted Wes. They came from down the creek and a lowing told him that cattle were being driven this way. This was cow country. But honest men generally drove their cattle by day! Wes reined to a stop, his mind sparked by suspicions.

It wasn't a big drive, he concluded after listening a minute longer. He was still in Pitkin County, but the Garfield County line lay only a mile or so ahead. He remembered a complaint sent a month ago from the sheriff of Garfield County to Sheriff Hooper at Aspen. The big grading contractors needed lots of fresh beef to feed crews. So petty rustlers sometimes drove small bunches of cattle south into mountain wildernesses of Pitkin County. There the beef could be butchered and peddled by the quarter to grading crews along the rail lines.

So this midnight drive would bear watching. Wes spurred to a cottonwood grove at a creek bend just ahead. He posted himself in tree shadows just off the trail. The drive came plodding on. Above the hoof sounds Wes caught the impatient command of a drover. "Get along there, bally."

A "bally" was a White-face; a Hereford. The stock was in sight now, moving sluggishly uptrail. Dim shapes in the dark. The shadows of this grove shut off moonlight, blotting out all detail except a whiteness of head and a blockiness of build. Then, as the drive came abreast of him, Wes noted one other thing which even night couldn't hide. These cattle were hornless.

Dehorning hadn't become a general practise on the west slope. Yet his own twenty heifers were dehorned. Also they were blocky Herefords. Three men rode back of them, one snapping a rope to haze the drive along. Under their droopy-brimmed hats the men were only silhouettes in the night.

As Wes made a quick count his suspicion hardened. Twenty head! Three men! He had three enemies down this way. The Ike Buford gang would have a double motive for driving off his stock. Profit and revenge.

In a rush of anger Wes whipped up his carbine and took aim on the middle rider. "That's far enough, Ike!" He sent a bullet over the man's head.

174

All three riders jumped their mounts into shadows beyond the road, each throwing a shot toward the flash of Wes Brian's carbine. Bullets chipped cottonwood bark on either side of Wes. He spurred Patch to one side, shouting, "Get 'em, Sheriff!" Aiming at sound and flash he fired twice again.

At the crackle of gunfire the heifers broke into a run. A mild lowing swelled to bellows as they stampeded up the valley.

More shots from across the trail made Wes shift his position. To make them think he was more than one he fired first with his forty-five and then with his rifle. "Head 'em off, Sheriff!"

Hooves splashed in riffles of the creek. When no more shots came Wes knew they were making off. They'd keep to the timber and he'd never find them in the dark. Probably they'd double back downstream to Satank, or perhaps to some hideout in Glenwood Springs.

Concern for his heifers drew Wes the other way. He found them a mile up Rock Creek, bedding down quietly by the trail. Well bred stock rarely stampeded and even when panicked wouldn't run far. Especially when the bunch was small. Wes made camp on the creek bank. "Come daylight, Patch, we'll drift 'em home."

The irony of it quirked his lips. Hunting for one enemy he'd bumped into another. Yet when he reported this to the law he couldn't swear who the three men were. He'd seen them only as hatted shapes in the dark.

175

At daybreak he drove his twenty heifers slowly down the trail. Seven miles took him to Rock Creek's junction with Roaring Fork. The town of Satank was milling with grading and bridge crews. Rails weren't here yet, because of uncompleted tunnels, and bridges. But the D & R G grade itself was finished to within twenty miles of Aspen.

In Satank Wes inquired at bars and stores. No one had seen the Buford gang lately. Nor anyone matching a description of Gil Dillon.

Wes drove his heifers on north over an oak ridge. From its top he sighted his Cattle Creek cabin. Everything looked peaceful. The cabin itself hadn't been raided. The wagon team grazed in the meadow.

After turning the heifers loose outside the fence, on government land, Wes fed and curried Patch. In the cabin he filled a coffee pot and opened his stove door to make a fire.

He was tossing in pine chips when an odd shape caught his eye. A brown cylinder which might have been a sliver of firewood — but wasn't. Wes plucked it gingerly from the grate and gave a grim inspection.

Someone had put a stick of dynamite in his stove.

Late in the afternoon he rode into Glenwood Springs and showed it to the Garfield County sheriff. The sheriff pooched out a lip. "Humph! Who'd want to blow you up?"

"Two outfits don't like me," Wes said. "One's the Ike Buford bunch. The other's Gil Dillon."

The sheriff nodded. "Sure. I read the papers. You knocked over Gil's brother Fred; and his pal Jenner. He'd want to get even, maybe."

"A man of his description rode down Rock Creek four days ago," Wes told him, "heading this way. I think it was Ike Buford who drove off my stock; and I think it was Gil Dillon who put dynamite in my stove."

"You *think* but you don't know," the sheriff said. "Unless you can swear under oath it was the Buford bunch, I won't bother to pick 'em up. I'll pick up Dillon, if I can, and hold him for Pitkin County. If you turn up anything new, let me know."

Wes stabled Patch and made a round of the Glenwood bars. The Buford gang came and went, he was told. They didn't keep rooms in Glenwood.

"They got a shack in the hills somewhere," a barman thought. "Just where I can't say. Every week or so they ride into some town and raise hell. Generally it's Frying Pan or Satank. Rowdy places, both of 'em."

"How long since you've seen Ike Buford?"

"Come to think of it, Ike was in here night before last. Came in for a rye highball just as I was closin' up."

"Alone?"

"Nope. Had a stranger with him. Short, heavy-set guy with a crack in his chin."

Gil Dillon had a cleft chin. "Did the heavy-set guy wear a black hat? Did he ride a brown horse? He had a bent nose and thick, black eyebrows?"

The barman screwed up his face thoughtfully. "He didn't bring his horse in with him. As for the rest of it, what you say fits him to a T."

Wes could hardly believe it. Was it an incredible coincidence? Gil Dillon and Ike Buford coming in here together? Yet why not? Wes Brian's run-in with Buford at Frying Pan had been in all the papers. And at a dozen bars Ike had sworn to get even. Gil Dillon would learn that much before he ever got here. And Gil too wanted to get even!

Gil and Ike had a common hate. What more natural than for Gil to look up Ike? Birds of a feather, that pair, each out to get Wesley Brian. After a few drinks they'd be ready for action. They'd cook up a scheme.

Like blowing me up with dynamite and driving off my stock!

To Wes it looked like plenty of hard riding in the days ahead. When he found Buford and company he'd find Gil Dillon with them. They'd get him, one way or another, unless he got them first.

Yet it was simpler this way. Now his troubles were all in one package.

CHAPTER
NINETEEN

Rufus Drake didn't look like a professional bodyguard. Except for his references, which were excellent, Bayard might have taken him for a college professor. The man wore no gunbelt. Only a slight bulge at the breast of his gray serge suit suggested a hidden holster. Tortoise shell glasses gave him an academic look. His build was slight and his speech mild.

He'd just arrived by stage and Bayard had met him at the Delmonico. Over coffee Bayard examined the references. Former clients included a Leadville silver king, a Wyoming cattle baron and a political boss in Chicago. Drake had also served as a detective on the Denver police force. Answering Bayard's inquiry he'd named a flat per diem rate and expenses.

"It's you I'm to protect?" he inquired.

"Later. But at the moment I'm under no threat." Bayard could be reasonably sure of that because Gleason would hardly kill a goose until the silver egg was laid. Only after the payoff would he be in any danger from the Ashcroft man. "But while I personally don't need protection at the moment, my secretary does. She saw a killer at his work. And he knows she saw him."

Drake nodded. "He's in town now?"

"I don't know. I don't even know who he is. As he fired at a man named Brian my secretary saw his face at a window. She'll recognize it if she ever sees it again. We think this same killer is the one who murdered a prospector on Piney Creek. If so he'd be ruthless enough to kill a witness."

Bayard gave a few more details, careful not to link himself to the killer. He made no mention of Gleason. "Miss Norman lives at the Clarendon. Better put up there yourself. She works an eight-hour day at my office, over the bank. If you can manage it, don't let her know she's being guarded."

"I know my business," Rufus Drake said quietly. "You have a personal interest in her, Mr. Bayard?"

The broker smiled. "Quite personal," he admitted frankly.

"She walks from the hotel to your office every day?"

"Yes. It's only three blocks. And when she goes out in the evening it's always with me." Bayard added with a bland confidence: "We're not engaged yet. But I think there's an understanding."

"She'll never know I'm watching her," Drake promised. He accepted a retainer check and left the restaurant.

Bayard went to his office and found Honora at her desk. "You just missed them," she announced mysteriously.

"Just missed who?"

"The most important clients we've had yet. Guess." Her use of the "we" sent a thrill through Bayard.

180

"Henry Gillespie, maybe? Or D. R. C. Brown?"

"Even more important than they are," Honora said, "Joshua B. Wilbur himself; and that Boston banker who represents a syndicate of investors."

"What did they want?"

"An appointment. I told them you'd be in at two o'clock."

They came promptly at two and Honora showed them into the private office. When they came out an hour later, Joshua Wilbur had a baffled look. An outburst from the Boston man floated back to Honora. "How much does the stubborn fool want, anyway?"

Then Frank Bayard appeared with something on his face Honora had never seen before. It seemed to be an odd mixture of elation and worry.

"They tried to buy me out. But I turned them down." Triumph was in Bayard's voice, yet Honora felt a flat note, somewhere.

"They offered a cool million," he told her, "for the *Lost Friend*."

At breakfast a morning later Honora read about it in the *Times*. Wilbur, the paper announced, had already sounded out the minority stockholders at Leadville. They'd promptly agreed to accept four hundred thousand for their forty percent. But the syndicate demanded all or nothing. An offer to buy out Bayard for six hundred thousand had been declined.

"And why not?" Bayard was quoted. "Right now the property's earning at the rate of a million per year. So the investment would net them a hundred percent the first year."

That day and the next the Wilbur offer dominated all talk around Aspen. "Bayard's crazy!" a shrewd veteran commented. "If it was me, I'd grab it. A vein of ore is like a woman; fickle. Here today and gone tomorrow."

The storm broke when angry minority stockholders arrived by stage from Leadville. All day Honora heard them arguing in the private office. Bayard resisted them stubbornly. Forty percent of the stock wanted to accept the offer; but sixty percent said no.

The minority group called in Chief Engineer Harv Random and asked his advice. Random gave it gravely within Honora's hearing. "If the stock were mine, gentlemen, I'd accept the offer."

"But why?" Bayard demanded. "In a year's time we'll get the million and still own the mine."

"Ore streaks have been known to play out," Random said. "Also there's a political consideration. Silver has enemies in Congress; enemies who'd like to repeal the Sherman Act or in some way put skids under bi-metallism. If that happens, the market for silver could hit mud bottom."

Then a messenger boy brought a sealed envelope with Bayard's name on it. Honora took it into the private office. She saw uneasiness in her employer's eyes as he read the note. Abruptly he reached for his hat and went out.

Frank Bayard found Gleason at the foot of the Abbey bar. "I got your note," he said sulkily.

"You gone loco?" Gleason demanded. "Turnin' down dough like that? Grab it and grab it quick."

"I can't. If you'll think it over you'll see why."

"To hell with why! A million's a million and I want my slice of it right now."

Bayard waited till the bartender was out of hearing. Then in a low, harassed voice he explained. "If I accept, I'd have to endorse the stock certificate over to the syndicate. Their lawyers would look at it, checking my title. They might notice something. Hang it, Gleason, I can't take a chance."

Gleason saw what he meant. "Yeh, you rubbed out Brian's name and wrote your own there. But hell, you've already recorded the transfer at the courthouse. It fooled the county clerk, didn't it?"

"Yes, but the clerk wasn't buying it for six hundred thousand. It was just a small routine stock transfer which he recorded in a book, then handed me back the certificate. As long as I own that stock, no other eyes need ever see it."

"What about that gal in your office?"

"She has access to the safe, naturally. But I keep the *Lost Friend* certificate in a private box at the bank."

"This erasure. How bad does it show?"

"A dim 'y' shows between the 'k' and the 'B' in my name. It wouldn't worry me except for that damned letter Hostetter wrote Brian. Brian showed it to Random. Neither of them can make anything out of it. But just one whisper about an erasure and they'll begin seeing daylight."

Gleason tossed down his liquor and gave an ultimatum. "Okay, Frank. Keep the damned stock if you want to. But I'm figurin' my cut on the basis of

183

Wilbur's offer. A third of your three-fifths. Which is two hundred thousand."

"Not while Brian's on the loose," Bayard said.

"You can kiss Brian goodbye. Two other parties are after him. Either they'll get him or I will. The day it happens I'll take my cut in cash. Or else!"

"Or else what?"

"I'll blow out of here and Harv Random'll get an unsigned letter from Chicago. It'll tell him you doctored a title and he'd better have the law take a look at it. That's the deal, pardner." Gus Gleason flung out of the bar.

As the final days of September slipped by, the search for Roger Norman exhausted itself and searchers drifted back to Aspen. The hue and cry for Gil Dillon faded. Without a dead man to confront him with, there was no real case against Gil. Only one searcher kept doggedly at it. Wesley Brian.

Early in October Honora got a letter from him. It was post marked Crawford, a cowtown on Smith Fork of the Gunnison.

". . . Almost caught up with Gil on Rock Creek . . . In Glenwood he hooked up with the Buford bunch and I figure they're running together somewhere. Buford's got some shifty cousins up Smith Fork, so I came over to see if they're holing up there . . . Say hello to Harv if you see him. And don't give up."

The letter didn't mention dynamite in a stove. Or a raid on Wes Brian's cattle. But the girl knew about those things. She read all the Glenwood and Aspen papers.

A sense of hopelessness settled over her. The reward offered by Bayard had brought no result. Nor had Wesley's persistent scouring of the mountains. How good they were to her, these two fine friends!

Today she was alone in the office and stood restlessly at a window. Across Galena Street she saw again the slim, well-dressed stranger with the tortoise shell glasses. Many times she'd noticed him there, idling in front of the Cowenhoven store. She'd seen him at the hotel too.

For something to do she opened the safe and made an inventory of the papers in it. Often she had to look for some security and she might as well know where everything was.

When she finished her list of the safe papers an odd fact struck her. Frank Bayard's certificate of *Lost Friend* stock wasn't there. All his other assets were; but not the *Lost Friend* stock.

A man's voice made her turn from the open safe. "Hi, Honora. Is the boss in?"

Harv Random had a report in hand. "The week's production figures," he announced. "Best tonnage we've had so far. Assays are holding up, too. Gosh! And in a month more we'll be shipping by rail! Maybe Bayard's right, turning down that Wilbur offer."

"He left for the day. I'll give it to him tomorrow." Honora took the report and put it in the safe.

Random sat down and filled his pipe. His frequent calls at the office had put him on familiar terms with Honora. "Heard anything from Wes Brian?"

"He's over in Delta County. Chasing another false alarm," Honora added with a sigh.

"That boy just won't give up, will he?"

"I almost wish he would," she said wretchedly.

Harv knew what she meant. Those lines of worry on her face weren't all for her father. "So do I, Honora. He'll get his head shot off one of these days, trailin' around after those rowdies."

The engineer puffed thoughtfully and then brought an old letter from his pocket. "Are you any good at puzzles?" he asked cryptically.

"I'm afraid not, Harv. That's the note poor Mr. Hostetter sent from Ashcroft, isn't it?"

"Wes asked me to figure it out for him. But I'm stumped. The stope roof was soft, all right. But why tell Wes about it?"

"Why indeed?" Honora wondered.

"So it's your turn now." Harv Random put the letter in her hand. "You're a smart girl. Set your pretty head to work on it. If you can't come up with anything, give it back to Wes next time he shows up in Aspen."

When he was gone, Honora puzzled over the letter. She noted the date, the postmark, the handwriting, the Covert House stationery.

Then a client came in to claim her attention. She put the Hostetter note in a safe pigeonhole, and locked the safe.

186

CHAPTER
TWENTY

Riding down Roaring Fork, Gus Gleason detoured both Frying Pan and Satank. It was a starlit night in mid-October. Most of the way he followed the new narrow gauge grade of the D & R G. Twice he detoured around construction camps. The Woody Creek bridge was just being started. Across the river, the Midland's standard gauge grade was a little ahead of the D & R G's. But the Midland had the worst bridge problems. Smart money was now on the Little Giant. Its first train, President Moffat assured everyone, would arrive in Aspen not later than November First.

All of which suited Gus Gleason. With everyone excited about the railroad race, there was less chance of some snooper stumbling upon the fraud of Frank Bayard.

In any case there was nothing in it for Gleason until Wes Brian was out of the way. That was the deal. It would take only one bullet and the bullet was in Gleason's saddle gun right now. On his last trip to Cattle Creek he'd failed to find his man home. So he'd put dynamite in the stove.

The trick hadn't worked. It must be a bullet after all. For weeks Gleason had kept away hoping that others would do the job for him. Gil Dillon was now hooked up with the Buford gang and all four were nursing grudges. With Brian in foolhardy pursuit of Dillon, a showdown gunfight had to Gleason seemed inevitable. There could only be one outcome. Four guns blazing at Brian would be a few too many.

But Brian had failed to catch up with them. And yesterday's papers said he was back in Glenwood Springs. So tomorrow he was sure to show up at his ranch for a look at his stock. Many things there would need his attention.

Day broke as Gleason passed Satank. Unseen, he left the river and turned north across a scrub oak ridge. Cattle Creek lay beyond the ridge and long ago Gleason had scouted the terrain there. He'd picked an exact spot to snipe from. He'd even picked a place to leave his horse.

But this time he wouldn't use a UT cartridge. The Hostetter inquest had warned him about the cartridge clew. So he'd switched to UMCs.

The sun was rising to his right when he reached the flat, timbered top of the ridge. Ahead he saw the oak thicket he'd picked to tie his mount in. Then a champing sound brought Gleason to a stop.

Dismounting, he advanced and peered warily into the thicket. *Four saddled horses were tied there.* The saddles had scabbards, but the scabbards were empty. It meant that four men had hidden their mounts here and gone on afoot with rifles!

After his first shock, a sly elation creased Gleason's face. Ike Buford, George Peck, Jakey Runkle and Gil

188

Dillon! Who else would sneak up on Brian! They too could read the papers. They too would figure he'd be home today.

For scouting purposes, Gleason had brought along a pair of field glasses. He'd used them twice before to watch Brian's cabin from a distance. To use them again he rode his horse a half mile up the ridge. A high, wooded butte bulged from it and he tied his mount at the foot, on its far side.

He'd be a fool to kill when others would do it for him. Those four snipers would wait patiently all day for Brian. And all day tomorrow if necessary.

They'd get him all right. One rifle might miss; but not four. Four bullets would sing a deadly volley. The only question was: when would it happen? This morning? This afternoon? Tomorrow?

The butte was well out of rifle range. But as a lookout it was perfect. Gleason took the field glasses from his saddle and climbed the steep slope afoot. The summit was brushy. He sat down with his back to a scrub cedar.

When he focused the glasses, the cabin seemed barely a hundred yards away. Every detail of it was clear. Closed windows and a smokeless chimney meant an empty house. A brown mound on the shed was stacked hay. Gleason's bullet, more than a month ago, had barely missed the stacker.

Shifting the glasses to the valley's near hillside, he picked up the snipers. From his high vantage he was able to spot them in a nook of brush. Four men. Three lay on their backs, hats over eyes. The fourth was watching the cabin. The range was about two hundred yards. It was almost the spot from which Gleason himself had fired.

The morning dragged. Twice the ambushers changed watch. At noon a canteen was passed from hand to hand. Gleason saw them open a ration sack. It all showed dogged patience and planning.

They're playing for keeps, Gleason thought. He curbed his own impatience and settled down to watch. A sure killing was on tap and he had a grandstand seat.

In early afternoon he saw a calico horse. It was far down the valley and coming this way. Brian! He was heading at an easy jog toward his cabin home.

The snipers had seen him too. Their lookout had alerted them. All four were kneeling in the brush, aiming rifles at the shed. Brian's first act would be to unsaddle there.

A neigh came from the calico as it sighted a work team in the pasture. One of the work team neighed back. Wes Brian waved his hat in the happy gesture of a long absent home-comer.

Gleason saw him stop at a fence. The rider leaned from his saddle to open a gate. Passing through onto his own land he spurred to a trot. He was in range now. Cocked death stared at him from the bores of four rifles.

As Brian drew up at the shed, Gus Gleason held his breath. He could see the four snipers with their rifles at aim. Why didn't they shoot?

190

There was plenty of time. Brian dismounted deliberately. He dropped the reins and stood by his horse while he rolled a cigaret.

He made a perfect target. From his distant lookout Gleason watched impatiently. Damn them! Why didn't they cut loose?

They didn't. They even lowered their rifles. A moment later Gleason knew why. They could see and hear something which was shut off from his own angle. Loping horses! The sound came from upvalley and presently two riders were in sight, heading toward Brian's cabin.

Two cowboys from the Circle Cross. The wind was just right to make their shouts reach Gleason. "Hi there, neighbor. We need a little help."

"We heard you was back, Wes," the other yelled. "Got any balin' wire?"

They stopped at the shed. "Blackleg epidemic up our way, Wes. Calves dyin' like flies!"

"We can save half of 'em, maybe, if we bleed dewlaps quick enough."

Under his breath Gleason cursed them. The snipers wouldn't shoot with Circle Cross men standing by. Circle Cross was a powerful outfit.

Blackleg, Gleason knew, was the scourge of the range when calves and yearlings were fall fat. Mature stock was usually immune. But death was sure and quick for a calf. The vets talked about a vaccine serum, but so far it was only talk. The common remedy was to stab a hole through the dewlap and tie a loop of baling wire through the hole. The wire kept the wound bleeding and kept the calf moving restlessly about. Movement and bleeding decreased the overfed sluggishness which brought on blackleg.

Evidently Brian had no bailing wire. For one of the Circle Cross men took off toward Glenwood Springs. The other, with Wes Brian riding at his stirrup, went loping upvalley toward the Circle Cross.

When they were out of sight, Gleason saw the four snipers quit the ambush and withdraw sullenly toward their horses. Gleason himself took another direction. When he was in the clear he veered toward Aspen.

Another trap had failed to catch Wes Brian. But although disappointed, Gleason was far from discouraged. Only a rare bit of luck had saved Brian. Those four killers meant business. They'd try again. Today was just a rehearsal. A postponement. Sooner or later they'd catch Brian at home and alone.

As the third week of October slipped by, Honora's last desperate hope dwindled. Day after day she sat in Bayard's office waiting for news which never came. The posted reward had brought not even a false alarm rumour. The last searcher was back from Conundrum Gulch. Even Wesley Brian had gone home.

On the twenty-second Honora got a letter from him.

. . . Just got home in time to help the Circle Cross bleed dewlaps. They want me to stay on a week longer and help them ship beef. They won't need to drive far this year. The narrow gauge is accepting shipments at Glenwood. And pretty

192

soon the Midland will be running trains up the Frying Pan.

I'm sorry I didn't catch up with Gil Dillon. I may yet because he's still on this range somewhere. Which is the main reason why I can't quite give up hope. Because if Gil has murder on his conscience, why hasn't he lit out for parts unknown? . . .

Honora tried to take comfort from it. But she couldn't. If her father had escaped from the Dillons, he'd make himself known somewhere. It was much easier to believe that he lay on the bottom of some pit or lake so deep that Gil Dillon had no fear he'd ever be found.

Restlessly, Honora opened the safe and took out the Hostetter letter to read and study again. Again she failed to explain it. She put it back in the safe and stood at the window, watching the ore wagons rumble down Galena Street. There was an endless procession of ore these days. They were stacking it along the narrow gauge right-of-way, ready to be loaded on cars. The day of shipping by wagon train was gone forever.

On the thirtieth the stages to Leadville and Granite and St. Elmo would make their last runs. November first would be the biggest day in all the history of Aspen.

Every man on the street knew it and excitement bubbled at every bar in town. The announcement was official now. On the first day of November a scheduled passenger train would arrive in Aspen. Governor Alva

Adams himself would be on it. A historic train coming to rescue Aspen from its winterbound, rock-walled isolation. Locomotive steam would puff new life into the town and ore shipments would triple. Profits would soar. Again the *Times* blared forth the same jubilant headline: TURN THE BOOM LOOSE AND LET 'ER RIP!

On the afternoon of the twenty-ninth Honora wrote a letter to Wesley Brian. She must thank him for his tireless search for her father.

Just as she finished it Frank Bayard came in flushed with excitement, two tickets in one hand and a roll of bunting under his arm.

"They've put me on the welcome committee," he announced. "Big doings, Honora. A parade and a banquet. Fireworks, floats, speeches, bonfires on the mountain. And only three days to get ready. I'll need your help."

"Of course. What shall I do?"

"First, you can make out place cards for the banquet. It will be at the Rink Opera House with seats for two hundred and fifty. Get that many cards and start with these names — the ones at the speakers' table. Give you the rest of them later." Bayard dropped a list on the desk. Topping it were the names of Governor Adams, Senator Teller and President Moffat of the D & R G.

"Jim Downing'll be toastmaster. These are for us, Honora." Bayard waved his pair of banquet tickets. "Be sure you don't seat us more than four chairs from the governor . . ."

"You'll meet the train, I suppose?"

"Of course. And you too. We'll meet the train and you'll ride with me in the first carriage behind the Flambeau Club. They'll march six abreast shooting off Roman candles. Be after dark when the train gets in. Lend me a hand, please?"

Honora helped him unroll his bunting. It was a huge banner with a rope threaded through a hemmed edge. Bayard tied one end of the rope to a cloak hook and threw the banner, rope and all, out a window. A man below caught it.

"Be right down," Bayard shouted.

He hurried to the street. From her window Honora saw them string the banner across Galena and toss the other end of the rope to a man atop the Cowenhoven store. The rope was tightened, hoisting the banner level with her window. Honora read the words — ASPEN WELCOMES THE LITTLE GIANT.

Cheers rang from the street as the banner went up. Others would go up on Mill, Hyman and Cooper. In the crowd Honora again noticed a slim, quiet man with tortoise shell glasses. He took no part in the cheering.

The girl addressed an envelope to Wesley Brian and put her letter in it. Then she decided she might as well return something which belonged to him. The mystery note from Ashcroft signed J. Hostetter. Both she and Harv Random had given up on it.

Honora unlocked the safe to get it. But it wasn't there! She knew exactly where she'd put it. The top, leftmost pigeonhole.

For a moment she felt only a mild puzzlement. Then a fact caught in her mind and clung there. Only two people could open this safe: herself and Frank Bayard.

Since she hadn't taken the missing paper from the safe, Bayard himself had taken it. Why?

Perhaps merely to study it as a puzzle. In that case he'd take it into his private office. Honora went in there for a look. The desk was bare. She looked in its drawers but failed to find the missing note.

The waste basket had scraps in it. The building's janitor emptied it only twice a week. On an impulse Honora put the basket on the desk and looked through it. One of the scraps was a small, charred triangle. Apparently it was the corner of a sheet which had been held between thumb and forefinger while the rest of it was held to the flame of a match.

This small, charred triangle had half a word on it. COV

The Covert House at Ashcroft! The Hostetter note was written on a letterhead of that hotel.

Honora's mild puzzlement changed to alert suspicion. Why would Frank Bayard burn the note? Only one answer made sense. He'd destroy it if he was afraid of it.

Why would he be afraid of it? It seemed to Honora that he'd be afraid of it only if it might embarrass or expose him.

Expose what? Guilt? The first question of all, the one which had hung unanswered all these weeks, reared up to challenge Honora. Why hadn't Hostetter written to Bayard instead of to Wesley Brian?

196

Was it because the man thought he'd sold his mine to Wes Brian? Until now Frank Bayard had been too far above suspicion to permit any such fantastic supposition.

Now it was different. He'd furtively destroyed the note. Other facts marshaled themselves before Honora. Bayard had sold land to Wes Brian for a three hundred dollar down payment. On about the same day Bayard for a like sum had bought the *Lost Friend* certificate from Hostetter! And why didn't Bayard keep that certificate in his safe, along with his other securities?

Honora locked the safe, tidied the desk, took her cloak and left the office. She hurried along a sidewalk crowded with celebrators and turned east on Cooper. At Hunter Street she went into the small front office of Colonel Willard's livery stable. "May I wait here, please, till Mr. Random comes down from the mine?"

She knew that Harv Random rode a horse daily back and forth to the *Lost Friend*. He kept the horse at Willard's. The late October dusk was closing in and Harv was sure to be here soon. Suspicions danced like imps through Honora's mind — suspicions she could confide only to Harv Random. Harv was her friend and Wes Brian's. Harv boarded at the Clarendon but they'd have no privacy there. Frank Bayard himself would breeze up, blond and hearty, to join them at supper. She'd better make Harv take her to the Delmonico. There, safe from the eyes and ears of Bayard, they must probe into a million dollar puzzle.

Did Frank Bayard, or Wesley Brian, really own the *Lost Friend* mine?

CHAPTER
TWENTY-ONE

Cooper Avenue was dark when Harv and Honora crossed it from Willard's barn to the Delmonico. They took a small table at the rear.

"Let's have it," the engineer demanded. "You look like you've been hit by an ore wagon."

She showed him a charred triangle of letterhead. In a rush of words she told him how and where she'd found it. He listened, the muscles of his lean face tensing as she voiced her suspicion. "What do you think?" she finished breathlessly.

For a while he sat grimly silent. Then he shook his head. "It explains what we couldn't explain before," he admitted. "It's solid as far as it goes — but it's not enough, Honora."

"Not enough for what?"

"Not enough to haul Bayard into court and make him show the certificate Hostetter endorsed. And even if it was enough, the demand would have to come from Wes Brian."

"I suppose you're right," Honora said. "And Wesley wouldn't demand it. He's not acquisitive."

"Just the same," Random followed up stubbornly, "three hundred dollars of his money passed through

Bayard's hands. And the same amount passed from Bayard to Hostetter. A little more than that sum was found on Hostetter's body. If we could only prove . . ."

"If we could only prove what, Harv?"

He didn't answer at once. At the front, on a stool at the snack counter, Honora noticed the slim man with the tortoise shell glasses. Late this afternoon she'd seen him across from her office window. It was almost as though he'd followed her here. But of course he hadn't.

"If we could only prove," Harv went on with shrewd, narrowed eyes, "that the three hundred dollars Wes handed to Bayard was part of the money found on the dead man! Remember that Hostetter sold his mine and left town two days *before* Bayard sold a piece of land to Brian."

To Honora it looked hopeless. "We can never prove it's the same money."

"We can't just let it drop," Random fretted. "If Bayard switched names on the certificate, it's a million dollar fraud. It might go even deeper. To murder! Somebody's been taking pot shots at Wes. Like the one through a kitchen window at the Clarendon."

The suggestion horrified Honora. "But Frank Bayard wouldn't do *that!*"

"No. But he could hire it done." An inspired gleam came to Harv's eyes as he leaned keenly across the table. "I just thought of something. A way to identify the money found on Hostetter's body."

She stared incredulously. "How?"

"I was on the coroner's jury at Hostetter's inquest. They showed us everything taken from his pockets. I had a good look at the money. Three hundred sixty dollars in tens and twenties."

A waitress came to serve them and Harv kept silent till she was gone.

"One of the tens," he remembered, "was an old banknote torn nearly in two. Someone had patched it with a strip of transparent tape. Wes might remember a patched tenner like that. If he left it with Bayard to invest, and if Bayard passed it on to Hostetter, and yet still later pretended to accept it as payment for land, then Bayard's a thief. He's guilty of the biggest mining fraud in the history of Colorado."

Honora looked at him, wide-eyed and almost afraid to speak. Other diners chattered around them and dishes clashed. The girl's question came so breathlessly that Random had to read her lips. "Should we tell the sheriff?"

"Not on a guess," Harv decided. "If it's a wrong guess it's not fair to wreck Frank Bayard's reputation. We can't do a thing till we've seen Wes Brian. The stake's too big. The scandal, if there is one, is too tremendous. We better not even consult a lawyer until we check with Wes."

"Check with him?"

"Yes. We can ask if he remembers a patched tenner in the money he handed Bayard."

"He's forty miles away."

"A day's buckboard drive if we get an early start." Harv's straight look challenged her. "Are you game?"

She didn't hesitate. "I can be ready at daybreak."

200

"Good girl." He stood up grimly. "I better take you home now."

They went out to the noisy street and he walked her to the Clarendon. "Keep away from Bayard," he warned.

"He'll wonder where I've gone."

Harv nodded thoughtfully. "So I'll drop a hint at the desk. You heard a rumour about your father, so I'm taking you to check on it. We'll be gone maybe two or three days. Okay? Now go straight to your room. Lock the door and get plenty of sleep. I'll have a fast rig here at six in the morning."

She came out in the gray dawn and Harv Random helped her into a two-horse buckboard. The team was Colonel Willard's best. Harv drove down Mill Street at a trot and at Main turned west on the Glenwood Springs road.

They crossed the Castle and Maroon Creek wagon bridges and came to the stalled end of a broad gauge grade. "This is what licked the Midland," Harv explained. "Girders for their last two bridges haven't come yet."

The rival road, following the other bank of Roaring Fork, didn't need to cross Castle and Maroon Creeks. Honora saw gangs of men over there; they were driving the final spikes on the narrow gauge rails.

On this side the trail ran between the Midland grade and the river. Construction wagons had cut deep ruts and the roughness slowed Harv to a walk. It was nearly two hours before he drew up at the Woody House, a roadside tavern at the mouth of Woody Creek. "Breakfast stop, young lady."

Beyond the trail was cluttered with traffic — construction wagons and ranchers heading for the big celebration at Aspen. Harv crossed the Tim Stapleton place, its stack pens bare. Most of the valley hay had been sold to the grading contractors. Below Tim's place, Snowmass Creek came in from the south and the Midland had a huge tie camp there.

Further on, tie-hauling wagons forced Harv's buckboard off the road. They had to bump along over sod. "Be dark when we get to Wes's place," Harv said.

At the noon stop, Frying Pan City was a milling bedlam. An army of track layers laid off by the D & R G were spending their pay. Harv drove by the Big Tent Saloon. "Wes had a fracas here one time."

Storeman Otto Schultz gave them a noon meal and fed the team. Driving on they followed Roaring Fork's north bank and along here the narrow gauge track was complete, every spike driven, ready for the first train day after tomorrow. They saw no more of the Midland's grade. Traffic petered out. But a local rain last night had muddied the road and again they were slowed to a walk.

Sundown caught them at Satank and Harv watered his team there. "If we were horseback," he told Honora, "we could cut north over a ridge and hit Wes's place in an hour. With a rig we got to go up Cattle Creek."

Five miles short of Glenwood they came to the mouth of Cattle Creek. Light was fading as Harv turned up it. "Hope Wes has supper ready. Hungry?"

"I'm starved," Honora admitted.

The trail ahead looked lonely and mysterious, the creek-bank cottonwoods looming dimly in the dusk. Dark closed about them as they passed a lightless cabin. "Wes said all his downcreek neighbors," Harv explained, "have hired out with their teams to the track camps."

The buckboard rolled on till a gate stopped it. Harv opened the gate and drove through. Further on a lighted window gleamed in the upcreek distance. "Here we are, Honora."

When Wes Brian heard them drive up he supposed it was someone on the way to the Circle Cross. Then a familiar voice hailed him. "Anybody home?"

He went out and the starlight showed him a buckboard. Its team stood with drooping heads as a man helped a girl from it.

As she turned her face he recognized Honora Norman. For a breath or two astonishment left him speechless. Only some big crisis could have brought her here. "It's about your father?" he asked. He took a small bag from her hand and saw that the man with her was Harv Random.

"No, Wes." It was Harv who answered. "It's about *you*. You and Frank Bayard. We think he slickered you out of a million dollar mine."

The facts and guesses came out, bit by bit, as Wes made them comfortable inside. The cabin had a kitchen, bunk-room and living room. They grouped in the kitchen while Wes warmed coffee and a leg of venison he'd roasted for his own supper.

"It boils down to this," Harv finished. "If we're guessing right you need a lawyer. Somebody to yank Bayard into court and put the fear of God into him; somebody who'll make him put that stock certificate under a microscope and see if the assignee's name has been tampered with. You want Jim Downing if you can get him. If he's too busy, maybe Porter Plumb'll go to bat for you."

A preoccupation grew on Wes Brian's face. He waited till he'd served them supper, then sat down with a cigaret. "Say that again, Harv. About the money you saw at a coroner's inquest."

"An old ten dollar bill," the engineer repeated, "was torn nearly in two and patched with a strip of tape. Patched on both sides. Do you remember anything like that in your wallet?"

An odd smile quirked Wes Brian's lips. "I sure do, Harv. So does Dave Coleman. And so does Jeb Slagle."

Harv gaped. "The devil you say? Who's Coleman? And who's Slagle?"

"Slagle," Wes told them, "is day bartender at the Buckhorn Saloon in Aspen. Dave Coleman is night shift foreman at the *Emma* mine. Dave and I made a ten dollar bet on the railroad race. Which I lost, because I bet on the Midland. We put up the stakes with Slagle at the Buckhorn bar."

Random's face fell. "That doesn't help. If you put up a patched bill, it's at the Buckhorn bar right now. So it couldn't have been in Hostetter's pocket."

Wes smiled cryptically. "You've got it wrong, Harv. Coleman and I each laid a ten dollar bill on the bar. Slagle took a look at mine and shook his head. 'It's kinda beat up,' he said. 'Let's have a good one,' so I picked up the patched bill and put another in its place."

Random digested it. Then he clapped Wes on the shoulder. He took Honora's hands and danced her about the kitchen. "It's the goods!" he crowed. "The goods on Bayard! He'll get fifty years in the pen and Wes'll get the *Lost Friend* mine."

His excitement was contagious and Honora caught the spirit of it. "To think we knew him, Harv, when he was only a stage driver!"

Wes made them sit down when he probed for weak spots. "You say Bayard burned the main piece of deadwood? That letter I got from Ashcroft?"

"But Honora and I saw it," Harv argued. "You saw it yourself. We've still got a burned corner. The very fact that Bayard burned it makes him look bad. He'll look still worse if that certificate shows an erasure."

"Do you think Mr. Downing will take the case" Honora asked.

"I hope so," Harv said. "He's tops."

Wes took a lantern and went out to the shed. He'd already fed the buckboard horses. Now he watered them and put them in shed stalls. To make room he turned his own calico loose in the meadow.

"Now look," he said when he went back into the cabin. "You've come forty miles and Honora's all tuckered. So get some sleep. You take the bunkroom,

Honora. Harv and I'll unlimber a bedroll in the front room."

They wanted to talk but he bullied them to bed. When lamps were out Wes lay on his back, with two blankets and a hard board floor under him, staring at a starlit square of window. A million dollar mine! He couldn't believe it. What would he do with a million dollars? Things like this didn't happen. He'd wake up and find he'd been dreaming.

But he didn't. When he wakened it was daylight outside. Harv Random slept soundly beside him.

Wes got quietly up, dressed, went to the kitchen and washed. He tiptoed about in his boots, hoping to have breakfast ready before the others were awake. That girl in there had another tough day ahead of her. The minute breakfast was over they must all hit the trail for Aspen to build a fire under Frank Bayard.

A bucket on the wash bench was half full. Another bucket, used for drinking water, was empty. Wes took it and stepped out the kitchen door. The well was in front, so he circled the cabin.

Just as he rounded the corner two rifle shots came from hillside brush across Cattle Creek. Bullets plunked into the cabin logs. Wes turned and dashed back to the kitchen door. Before he could get through it, two more shots came from an opposite direction. A bullet nicked Wes and drew blood.

He stumbled inside, slammed and bolted the door. Harv's voice called from the front. "What's all the shooting about?"

206

Wes had ideas but no time to talk. At least four riflemen were out there. They thought he was alone here and they'd come to kill. He heard Honora stir in the bunkroom. Her fate was linked with his own now. Four more shots came, two from the hillside, two from a post pile in the meadow. The meadow shots splintered through the kitchen door. Wes picked up his saddle gun and stood grimly at bay.

CHAPTER
TWENTY-TWO

Random had brought no gun along. He had no skill with firearms. But he accepted a forty-five Wes gave him and took a post under the creekward window. "Take a peek every once in a while, Harv. Sing out if they charge the cabin."

A step made Wes turn and he saw Honora in the inner doorway. She was fully dressed, her face pale as she looked at Harv's gun. "Do you have one for *me?* I can shoot too."

"Get back!" Wes yelled as another bullet zinged in and thudded through a wall board. He pushed the girl back into the bunkroom where the only window faced downcreek. From that direction there'd been no shots.

"Is it the same man?" she asked Wes. "The one who fired into the hotel kitchen?"

"He might be one of 'em. But I doubt it. More likely it's the Buford bunch and Gil Dillon. They add up to four." Wes went into the cabin's kitchen and looked out. A rifle barrel and a hat showed above the post pile in the meadow.

He pushed his own piece through the window and fired. A puff of smoke bloomed on the post pile as the man fired back. The hat disappeared.

Honora called from the bunkroom. "Do they think you're alone, Wesley?"

"Likely. They must've come during the night." Wes raised his voice. "Don't let 'em sneak up on you, Harv."

"What about your neighbors upcreek?" Harv called back. "Any chance they'll come along?"

"The Circle Cross? They shipped a trainload of beef to Denver yesterday. The whole outfit, except a cook and a chore man, went with it." Probably it explained why Buford and Dillon had timed their attack for today. Not until today could they be sure that friendly neighbors wouldn't ride by. And until yesterday Wes himself had been at the Circle Cross, helping them bleed dewlaps and drive beef to the cars.

Honora's calm voice made him turn. "May I have this?" She'd come into the kitchen with a single-barrel shotgun.

"No shells for it," Wes said. He'd borrowed it from the Circle Cross cook to hunt ducks with, but as yet hadn't bought any ammunition. "There might be a shell in the chamber. I haven't looked."

He took the shotgun and broke it at the hinge. The brass end of a shell showed at the breech. This weapon had no magazine. "You could blast once with it, but that's all."

Wes shoved a chair back of the stove and made her sit in it. There a slug through the window wouldn't hit her. The log walls were bulletproof. He gave her the shotgun, warning her again that she couldn't shoot but once. "Hold your fire unless they crash in on us."

Then rapid firing and a yell from the front made Wes rush in there. He found Random blasting with his revolver through the creekward window.

"They started at me," Harv reported, breathing hard. "Like to scared me to death. Two of them with rifles. Broke out of brush over there. Crossed the creek and came running toward the cabin."

As Wes looked out, he was in time to see two men dive into oak brush beyond the creek. "When they saw me at the window with a gun," Harv said, "they turned and ran. I sure thought I was a goner."

"Until you popped up," Wes concluded, "they figured I was alone here. They heard me shoot from the kitchen so they thought this side was unguarded."

Harv brightened a little. "So now maybe they'll ride off and leave us alone."

"Maybe. But I doubt it. It'll make 'em careful, that's all."

"This trigger sure pulls hard. I had to use both hands to shoot."

"Have you reloaded?"

A sheepish look on the engineer's face admitted that he hadn't. "Then cram in some more shells." Wes thumbed toward a box of forty-five cartridges.

As Random reloaded, Wes went back to the kitchen. To his complete shock he found Honora standing in the open rear door with a shotgun in her hands. She wasn't aiming it. She merely posed in the doorway a moment, then stepped back, slamming the door shut.

Two bullets from the post pile splintered through it.

210

"Are you crazy? Showing yourself like that?" Wes pushed the girl to her seat back of the stove.

"I thought perhaps they'll go away," she explained simply, "if they know I'm here."

"They won't. They've gone too far. We've seen them. And for all they know they've already hit one of us." But the sheer courage of Honora made Wes humble. He poured water into a cup and dipped the corner of a towel into it. "We've got to make it last," he said gently.

She looked at the buckets, one empty, one half full. "Is it that bad?" she murmured in dismay.

He nodded. As she wiped her eyes with the moist towel he added: "We've drinking water for a day and a half, maybe. Our only chance is to stand 'em off till someone comes by."

After another look out the window he fired the kitchen stove. "We've got bread, bacon, canned beans and a sack of piñon nuts."

"And coffee," Honora said.

"No. Coffee boils away water and every drop counts."

When bacon was sizzling he again looked from the window. In clear sunlight he saw two faces peering over the post pile. He threw a shot at them and they ducked out of sight. "One of 'em's Gil Dillon. Other calls himself Peck. That leaves Ike and Jakey on Harv's side." Wes raised his voice. "How you making out, pardner?"

"They're behaving themselves," Harv called back.

"They know we're short of water," Wes reasoned. "They saw me start to the well with an empty bucket. So they just have to keep us penned up."

Two shots from Random's side brought a crash of glass and thuds at an inner wall. "I raised up for a look," Harv said hoarsely, "and they cut loose. The same two men."

Wes put bread, bacon and a cup of water on a plate. "Take it to him, Honora. And stay out of line with the windows."

While she was gone he weighed the chances. His down-creek neighbors were hauling ties for the Midland. The sound of gunfire wouldn't carry upcreek to the Circle Cross. Only a cook and a chore man were there. A bare chance that one of them might ride this way today or tomorrow.

Wes fed himself sparingly and filled a plate for Honora.

Spasmodic fire came all through the day. "They're just pinning us down," Wes concluded. "Maybe they figure to raid us tonight. Anyway they can keep us awake. We can't hold out without sleep and water."

"They can sleep and we can't," Harv agreed.

"But aren't they taking too big a risk?" Honora puzzled. "Just for revenge and hate?"

"Revenge and hate go a long way," Wes argued, "if you're mean enough. They hate me all right. Gil because I gunned his brother. The Buford bunch because I spoiled their fun one time; and later caught them stealing cattle. I can't identify them in court; but they think I can. They figure I can send them to the pen. So they're out to get me, all four of 'em. They didn't figure on you and Harv bein' here."

212

"That face at the hotel kitchen window!" the girl brooded. "You're sure it wasn't one of these four men?"

"It was the man who killed Hostetter. A guy who used UT shells. Call him Mr. UT."

"You've never quarreled with UT," Honora reasoned. "So *his* motive can't be revenge or hate. Nothing's left except money."

Wes grinned. "I didn't know I had any — until you told me about Bayard gypping me out of a silver mine."

"That's just it!" Honora put in shrewdly. "As the victim of his swindle, you're dangerous to Bayard."

Wes thought it over and nodded soberly. "Could be. Bayard's no gunman himself, so maybe he hires Mr. UT to fix both me and Hos . . . Down!"

He made her stoop below the window level as a fusilade of shots poured in. They came from the post pile. "Those fellas've got magazine repeaters."

At intervals during the afternoon similar volleys came from Random's side of the cabin. "Keep down!" Wes kept warning. "We've got to wait it out. And stay awake all night. Sky's clear, so we'll have moonlight. That might keep 'em from raiding us."

By dusk, neighs of distress were coming from the shed. The buckboard team hadn't been fed or watered all day. "They'll break out," Wes predicted. The shed door was closed but not locked; and the horses weren't haltered to their stalls.

Just after nightfall they heard the shed door kicked open. Two horses trotted out and made for the creek.

★   ★   ★

Wes lighted no lamp. Half the night went by without a besieging shot. Honora began to hope they'd gone away. Wesley Brian knew better. "They want us to think that. They're lying doggo to cut us down if we make a run for it."

"How's the water?" Harv asked.

"Only a quart left."

Another silent hour crept by. Moonlight touched the meadow and showed a grazing calico horse. "They're gone," Harv said hopefully.

"They're teasing us," Wes insisted. He made Honora go to the bunkroom and try to sleep.

During all the darkness not a shot was fired.

When light was good enough to shoot by, Wes joined Harv briefly at the creekward window. He aimed his rifle through it and sent four bullets into oak brush on the hillside.

"They're still there, Harv."

"How do you know?"

"My shots came just close enough to make them change position. I saw boughs shake in two directions. One moved to the right, one to the left."

Harv looked into the bunkroom, then turned with a grim smile. "She's asleep, Wes."

"Good. Let's not wake her." Wes went back to his post in the kitchen. His shot from the window drew answering fire from the post pile. "They're still out there. Breakfast, Harv?"

"You can skip that salty bacon. Makes me too thirsty."

214

"We've got water till noon," Wes calculated. He traded another shot with the post pile. Then he heard a wry laugh from Random.

"I just thought of something, Wes. This is the day the first train runs into Aspen. So we miss the big celebration. Bonfires and Roman candles. Everybody happy but us!"

"And I," Honora exclaimed from the bunkroom, "am supposed to make out place cards for the banquet! Dear, dear! What *will* they do?"

In a little while she came out with a forced smile on her pale, strained face. She'd slept in her clothes and her hair was disordered. "Don't show me a mirror. I couldn't bear it!"

Wes gave her a sip of water and she eyed the rest of it wistfully. "It would make one cup of coffee apiece!" she sighed.

"You get nothing but well water, lady. A drop at a time."

As the light broadened the enemy began firing angrily from both sides. "Getting impatient and jumpy," Wes concluded. "They're afraid someone might happen by."

"They didn't figure it would take this long," Harv agreed.

The persistent firing kept up for another hour. Evidently the war of nerves was taking an equal toll from the besiegers.

"Is there any real chance," Honora asked, "of anyone coming by?"

"Sure there is. The Circle Cross boys might come home from Denver." But Wes Brian knew they wouldn't. Not during the short time they could hold out.

Honora read the truth in his eyes. "You're not fooling me, Wes Brian. It would take a miracle and you know it."

"A *miracle*, did you say?" The voice was Harv's from the front room. "Maybe we've got one. Listen."

All they could hear was gunshots.

"Sounds like one of them shifted position," Wes said. "He's firing from down the creek."

"His rifle's got a different sound," Harv thought. "Listen."

"By golly you're right!" Wes looked out at the post pile. The men behind it were firing — but not at the cabin. Puffs of smoke answered them from a cottonwood grove down the creek.

"Hooray!" Harv cheered. "We've got a friend down there. Somebody came along and cut loose on them."

The shriek of a bullet-hit man proved it. Wes saw Peck pitch into sight from behind the post pile. The posts gave no protection from downcreek fire. The man fell forward and lay still.

At the same minute Gil Dillon deserted his shelter and raced across the meadow, away from the cabin. Bullets kicked dust at his heels as he ran toward a calico horse.

Wes took aim over the sill and fired. He missed. But his next shot dropped Gil face-down in the hay stubble out there.

216

"There goes Ike Buford!" Harv yelled. "Bring your rifle, quick!"

Wes dashed to the front room but was too late. "They took off," Harv reported breathlessly. "Both of them. Someone opened up from the grove downcreek and it smoked 'em out. I saw Ike and Jakey crash uphill through the brush."

"They've got horses on the ridge, likely. Who's that coming?"

A mounted man rode out of the grove, a carbine balanced across the pummel of his saddle. He was a man of slight build wearing tortoise shell glasses and a soft felt hat.

As he dismounted in front, Wes and Harv went out to meet him. "Is Miss Norman all right?" the man inquired anxiously.

"She is. But who are *you?*"

"I'm her bodyguard," the man announced with a half shy smile. "Drake's the name. Rufus Drake."

CHAPTER
TWENTY-THREE

"Wait till I draw a bucket of water," Wes said. "Then we'll make a gallon of coffee."

While Honora made the coffee, the three men went to the hillside thicket from which Ike Buford and Jakey Runkle had retreated. Empty rifle shells were scattered about the spot. None of them were UTs.

"We hit one of them." Wes pointed to a bloodstained rag.

The hit couldn't be very serious, since both men had gone uphill at a run. By now they'd be a long way off on horseback. "Following them is a sheriff's job," Wes decided.

They recrossed the creek and went out into the meadow. At the post pile they found Peck. Gil Dillon lay a short distance further on and both men were dead.

One by one they were carried to the shed and covered with a wagon sheet.

At the cabin Honora was waiting with a pot of coffee. "So it's *you!*" she exclaimed after a close look at Rufus Drake. He was the man who'd so often idled across from her office window.

When they were comfortable, Drake explained. "Frank Bayard brought me from Denver. I'm a professional bodyguard. He expects to need protection himself, later; in the meantime he asked me to guard Miss Norman."

"From whom?" Honora asked.

"From the sniper you saw at a hotel window. I believe the man took a shot at *you*, Mr. Brian."

"Twice," Wes said. "And once at John Hostetter. We call him Mr. UT. Did Bayard mention his name?"

The guard shook his head. "But I think I know who he is."

"Yes?" Wes prompted.

"As her guard I naturally followed Miss Norman back and forth between the hotel and her office. Being a block behind her I saw things she couldn't see. One day a man ducked into the Brick Saloon to keep her from seeing him. A few days later the same man did it again. So he might be the window sniper. I looked him up."

"Who is he?"

"An Ashcroft saloonman named Gus Gleason. I asked Marshal McEvoy if he has a police record. McEvoy says the man was fined fifty dollars late in August for disturbing the peace. Seems some drunk broke a bottle over his head and Gleason chased him up the street, shooting at him. But he didn't hit the man."

Wes popped his hands together with a sudden memory. "I knew I'd seen that window face somewhere! He came running out of the Buckhorn Bar

219

and took off up Hyman. It was dark and I didn't get a very good look."

"According to McEvoy," Drake went on, "he's known as Gus the Grubstaker. Last man he grubstaked was Hostetter — later found shot dead."

Honora was bursting with curiosity. "How did you find me, Mr. Drake?"

"I bungled it," the guard admitted. "I saw you meet Mr. Random at a restaurant. You seemed excited — like you were cooking up something. When Mr. Random picked you up in a rig at daybreak next morning, frankly I thought it was an elopement. I had to be sure, though. That was my job. So I hired a saddle horse and tagged along."

"And lost us where?" Harv prodded.

"In the dusk at the mouth of Cattle Creek. I thought you'd gone on into Glenwood Springs. Spent all day yesterday looking for you there. Finally found a man who saw a buck-board turn up Cattle Creek at dark day before yesterday. I asked who lived up Cattle Creek. He named Wesley Brian. The name connects with Gleason's in two ways: Gleason grubstaked Hostetter and Brian found the body; both Brian and Hostetter were shot at with UT shells." Rufus Drake lighted a pipe, puffed it to a glow. "So here I am."

"What you don't know," Harv told him, "is that your boss Bayard is a thief. That's the way it figures. Listen." In precise terms he outlined the case against Bayard.

Drake listened intently. He asked a few sharp questions. He looked at a charred scrap of letter. He'd been a policeman and he had a policeman's wit. In the

220

end he was convinced. "If I'd known, I wouldn't have hired out to him."

"Lucky for us you did," Wes said.

"Anything I can do," Drake offered, "to help clean up this mess?"

Harv Random answered him. "Yes. Take care of this end of it. I mean get the sheriff out from Glenwood and let him take over." The engineer looked at a wall clock. "The rest of us have just got time to catch a train at Satank."

"What train?"

"The first train to Aspen. Today's November first," Harv reminded them. He turned grimly to Honora. "Frank Bayard's on the reception committee, you said? Good! So we'll be on the train and let him receive us!"

Drake smiled shrewdly. "If he's hooked up with Mr. UT, spiders'll crawl down his spine when he sees the three of you get off that train together."

Honora stared. "You mean . . . ?"

"Figure it out yourself," Drake said. "Hostetter's main contact at Ashcroft was Gleason. He'd just transferred a title to Brian. So if he mentioned Brian's name to anyone, it would most likely be to Gleason."

"That ties the threads!" Harv broke in. "So when news of the *Lost Friend* bonanza broke, Gleason made a deal with Bayard. For a split, he'd handle the two dangerous witnesses."

Wes stood up, haggard and unshaven, thumbs in his gunbelt. "So what are we waiting for? Hurry and get ready, Honora, or we'll miss the train to Aspen."

The train was hours late getting started from Glenwood Springs. At first it was to be ten coaches long, then twelve, then fifteen. But more and more people wanted to go. News of the big celebration had spread all along the Western Slope. No one wanted to miss the biggest fireworks display, and the most extravagant parade of floats, ever to be staged in Colorado.

Twenty coaches were hooked on, and finally twenty-five. Two doughty narrow gauge locomotives puffed at the head; and at the rear was coupled President David Moffat's palatial private car, the *Columbine*. Distinguished guests in it included Senator Teller and Governor Alva Adams. A band at the Glenwood depot saw them off.

They were far behind schedule but no one cared. It was forty miles upgrade to Aspen and the overloaded engines barely crawled. And still no one cared. It beat stagecoaches and wagons. Until today, wooden wheels were all this valley had ever known. A thousand cheering passengers made the ride and guns were fired from the coach windows. "Everybody rides but the sheriff!" "Aspen, here we come!"

In late afternoon the train stopped at Satank. Two men and a girl were waiting to get on there. "We're full up," the conductor told them. "Every seat taken."

Honora looked in dismay at the crowded coaches. Then Jack Carson of the Carson Stage Line poked his head out a window. "That's Wes Brian," Carson yelled. "Let him on, Conductor. He can have my seat. We need him in the parade."

222

Wes refused to get on without Honora and Harv. A way was made for them and they squeezed into the first coach. Immediately Phil Carbury, who ran the Aspen bookshop, got up and gave his seat to Honora. In the aisle Carson pounced on Wes Brian. "You're the answer, boy!" he exclaimed jubilantly.

"The answer to what?"

"You remember Walt Goff? He drove the first stage over Independence Pass, back in '81. He's retired now. Lives in Glenwood and I went down there to get him. The reception committee wants him to drive the governor from the depot to the hotel. In the very same stage he drove over the pass in '81. A six-in-hand, three gray horses on one side and three blacks on the other."

"A right smart outfit," Wes agreed. "And Walt sure rates the job of driving it."

"But he's laid up and can't come. So what about you, Wes? Next to Walt Goff, you're the most famous driver I ever had. The coach'll be at the depot. All you got to do is climb up there and grab the reins."

Wes looked dubiously at Honora. "Should I?"

"Of course you should," she decided promptly. Wes was still haggard but no longer unshaven. They'd all freshened up before leaving the cabin.

Carson gave her a close look and remembered. "You were on the driver's seat with him, weren't you, when Lockwood held up his stage?"

"She sure was," Wes said proudly. "And she stayed right there till I unloaded her at the Clarendon."

"Do it again!" A new idea struck the stage line operator. He was a natural showman. "If there's one thing more needed to make people look at that stage, it's a pretty girl sitting by the driver. How about it, Miss Norman? It's just from the depot to the hotel."

"Which is where she's going anyway," Wes grinned.

"I'm not dressed for it!"

But Honora's protest was overruled. "It's an historic event," Carson argued. "The governor and his staff inside; a famous driver and his gal outside. Now come on back to Mr. Moffat's car and meet the governor."

He took Honora's hand and led her down the aisle. Wes and Harv followed. The train was moving, crawling slowly up the river bank toward Aspen.

A medley of greetings reached Wes. "Hi, Snapper!" "Ever ketch up with that Dillon fella?" "Good thing you quit skinnin' a stage and tuk up ranchin'. Next stage you see'll be in a museum!"

They went on down the train, passing from coach to coach. The sway as they crossed the open vestibules made Wes take Honora's other hand. Every seat in every coach was filled with excursionists bound for Aspen.

"It's a long walk, Miss," Carson said. "But we're halfway there. Only ten more coaches to go through."

But there weren't ten more. Not for Honora Norman. There weren't any more at all. This coach was as far as she ever got down the train.

She stood transfixed in the aisle, staring into a pale, hollow-eyed face. Wes followed her gaze to a thin, gray-haired man who seemed vaguely familiar. Beside him sat a stocky man with a powder-pitted face and the hands of a hard rock miner; he also seemed oddly familiar.

Honora's eyes were only for the older man. "Dad!" She threw her arms around him. "Dad, dear!"

"He's been plenty sick, lady. Here, take my seat." The stocky man got up and made Honora take his place. "Go ahead and make a fuss over him. He needs it. And I reckon you do too," he added as tears welled in Honora's eyes. "He had a real tough time of it, up there in that gulch."

Wes and Harv drew the man down the aisle a little way. "I've seen you before, haven't I?" Wes asked.

"Likely. If you're from Aspen. I'm Clyde Waring. Used to own a fourth of the *Little Lucy*."

Wes remembered. The *Times* had made a human interest story out of it. The *Little Lucy* was a third rate claim up Hunter Creek. "Let's see'f I've got it right. You had three lazy partners. They played the dives and made you do all the work. One day you got fed up and quit them. Told them you'd give your share to the first bum you met on the street. Which you did as you passed through town."

Clyde Waring glanced over his shoulder at Honora. She was holding her father's thin cheeks tenderly between her hands. They saw her kiss his lips. "Roger Norman was grateful," Waring explained in a lowered voice. "He wrote me a letter of thanks. He said I was the only man in Aspen who'd been kind to him. He said it meant a lot because he could send what I'd given him on to his daughter. She'd respect him for it and that meant still more, because his self respect was all

225

gone. He wrote me all that in a letter and I answered him. That's how he knew where to find me."

"And where," Wes queried, "*did* he find you?"

"At my new claim in Queen Basin, just east of Gothic."

Wes exchanged quick looks with Random. Both knew that Queen Basin was just across the range in Gunnison County, and by crow-flight not more than ten miles from the head of Conundrum Creek in this county. Yet an all but impassable divide lay between.

"How he got over it we'll never know," Waring said. "He was crazy with fright; thought the Dillons would catch him unless he kept going. He must have gone over Triangle Pass. Once I killed a mule on that climb. Norman had to fight his way through brush and live on berries. But he got over the hump, some way. He was skin and bones, ragged and hairy, when a sheepherder found him at the top of Copper Creek. He asked where Clyde Waring's claim was. The herder knew and brought him to me."

"Why didn't you report it?"

"For a long time I didn't know who he was. He looked like the wild man of Borneo. He was half out of his head and burning up with mountain fever. Finally I shaved his face and saw a sabre scar; then I knew he was the man I'd given a piece of the *Little Lucy* mine."

"Don't you read the papers?"

Waring shrugged. "Not often. Frankly I thought he was running from the law. Felt sorry for him and didn't want to turn him in. Bit by bit he picked up. Then I got

226

hold of a Gothic weekly and read about the Dillon case in Aspen."

"You were only thirty miles from Aspen."

Waring nodded. "Thirty miles by mule and two hundred by rail. So we came by rail."

Evidently they'd ridden the Crested Butte branch down to Gunnison. And from there come over Marshall Pass to Salida; from there up through Leadville and Tennessee Pass; then down Eagle River to Glenwood just in time to catch the first train to Aspen.

"Which reminds me," Harv put in. "There's a five thousand dollar reward posted at the Aspen bank. All yours, Waring."

There was a pretty justice in it, Wes thought.

Waring looked sideways at Roger Norman and lowered his voice. "A package of good came out of it that you wouldn't expect. He's cured, far as I can tell. Seems like starvation and fever just naturally burned it out of him."

"You mean his yen for liquor?" Harv asked.

"Seems like it. In all the time he's been with me he hasn't touched it. He's had plenty of chances, but nary a drop."

Wes looked from the coach window and saw that night had fallen. They'd passed through Frying Pan and he could see the lights of Snowmass across the river.

"Let's go see what the argument's about," Harv said.

Honora, sitting by her father, seemed to be resisting persuasive talk by Jack Carson. Moving nearer they heard the stage line man say: "But you promised! It's all set up."

The girl linked her arm snugly through Roger Norman's. "Do you think I'd leave my father! Just when I've found him!"

"It's only while you ride from the depot to the hotel," Carson pleaded. "Look. We've a dozen extra guest carriages. The Major can ride in one of them with Random and Waring. Or anyone else you want . . ."

"No," Honora said serenely. She looked fondly at her father, her eyes blue and shining with the joy of reunion.

Then Roger Norman himself settled it. He was surprisingly firm. "Do as he says, Honora. It's planned and I don't want to spoil any plans. I'll be proud to see you ride in the governor's coach."

"Of course, Dad. If you want it that way."

But she refused to go with them to the private car. Wes and Harv went along with Carson and met the distinguished company there. When they returned to the Normans the train had crossed Woody Creek and was on the last lap of its run.

The cheering stopped. No more six-guns were fired from the coach windows. A hush came over the crowded cars. Fish-plates clicked under the wheels and the little engines puffed mightily up the Roaring Fork grade. But from a thousand passengers came hardly a sound, those last few miles. Something big was about to happen in their lives.

A single voice spoke. "Keep your ears open, Jake!"

They listened, heard only the hum of wheels and the chug of engines. Dark, piney hills hemmed them on either side.

228

The train rounded a curve and the valley widened.

"Look!" a man said hoarsely. "There she is, boys! All lit up like Christmas!"

They crushed toward the right hand windows. And still there was relative quiet through the coaches. An imminence of impending drama had laid hands on them. The curtain was up, now, and there lay Aspen with every light burning; above it a hundred bonfires blazed on the shaft-pitted slope of a mountain.

An old miner spoke from the seat in front of Honora's. "It ain't like the first time I came in here — afoot on snowshoes — pullin' a grub sled over the pass."

"Look! Kinda purty, ain't it?"

Reds and blues and greens and yellows streaked the sky. Rockets and Roman candles made star-spangled arcs over the town.

"Listen, Jake! Sounds like giant powder."

Thundering salutes came from the mountainside mines. The train was close in now, chugging across Roaring Fork bridge. Coach windows rattled as blast after blast rocked the train. Dynamite and giant powder. Roars from Smuggler Mountain vied with even mightier roars from the Silver Queen herself — from the *Molly Gibson* on one side to the *Spar* on the other.

Then shouts of welcome from the waiting town. Band music blared brassily at the depot.

"Here we are, Jake."

Jake turned his grizzled face to grin back at Honora. "It sure beats a mule, don't it, lady?"

CHAPTER
TWENTY-FOUR

The parade formed along Frances Street, at the foot of Mill. A reception committee had led the governor and his staff to an ancient stagecoach; other important guests were led to waiting carriages.

As Wes handed Honora up to the stage's high, front seat, the same question puzzled them both. She'd asked it twice since getting off the train and Wes had no answer. "Where is Frank Bayard?"

All of Aspen was here — except its newest silver king. He was on the reception committee. The other committeemen had all appeared with hearty greetings. Mayor Harding, Sheriff Hooper, Marshal McEvoy, Editor Wheeler and Attorney Jim Downing. Everybody joyously on hand — except Frank Bayard.

As Wes climbed up and took the reins, Honora gave a nervous laugh. "I just remembered, Wes. I've a date with him to ride in a parade carriage; just behind the Flambeau Club, he said. And a date for the banquet, too. Only four chairs from the governor, he said."

On the depot platform Mayor Harding was making a speech. "I have the distinguished honor, fellow-citizens, to present to you the Denver and Rio Grande Railroad. And to announce our emancipation from snow drifts

230

and craggy trails, an end to eight years of tramping and teaming over the passes, a final blessed rescue from the miseries of wilderness isolation . . ."

Cheers and a thunder of explosions drowned him out.

Marshal McEvoy, after dashing back and forth on a bay stallion, gave the order to march.

The parade headed up Mill Street led by mounted police in platoon formation. Back of it marched the Flambeau Club, each man with a sack of Roman candles and showering the street with spouts of colored stars.

"It's beautiful!" exclaimed Honora. Beyond, bonfires and rockets still shot skyward from the mountain mines.

Committeemen in open carriages followed the Flambeau Club. Then came the Aspen Rifles under Captain Gosline, just home after subduing Colorow's Utes, now marching as a guard of honor to Governor Alva Adams.

Then a stagecoach with a slim, gunslung driver at the reins and with a lovely, auburn-haired girl by him. From the coach the governor waved to the crowd. Wes Brian held his reins high and proudly, a six-in-hand with three grays on one side and three blacks on the other. The stage itself was ancient and rickety, the symbol of an era now ending. A banner across its baggage boot told its epic story: THE FIRST — AND LAST — STAGE TO ASPEN.

Behind it came other guests in carriages — President Moffat and Senator Teller. Then the Cowenhoven

Volunteer Fire Department. Finally a feature widely publicized as the Transparencies.

Looking back, Honora tried to make them out. They were still life tableaux borne on wagon frames, each posed behind lighted mosquito netting. The first was an ore-laden burro labeled: A FREIGHT TRAIN of '86. The next, called AN ARMSTRONG HOIST, showed a miner at a shaft windlass.

Crowds on either side cheered wildly. "Drive 'em pretty, Wes." "Howdy, Governor." "Don't let them fellers in Washington put the skids under silver, Alva." "You sure picked a good lookin' gal, Snapper."

Honora laughed. "I feel like I'm in a gold fish bowl."

Wes turned a sober face to her. "Forget those jokers and think about Bayard. Where the dickens is he, anyway?"

At Main the parade turned west to Monarch, then south on Monarch to Hyman, then east on Hyman. People thronged every walk. It seemed that of all Gilpin County only Frank Bayard wasn't in or watching this parade.

Bayard and one other. "I haven't seen that Gleason man either," Honora said.

"You won't," Wes predicted. "We saw him at a window, so he's not going to let us see him again. But Bayard? He's a crook, sure. But he doesn't know we know it."

"He may suspect we know," Honora reasoned. "With Harv Random, Rufus Drake and me all leaving town suddenly. And coming back with you. Maybe he saw us get off the train and was frightened."

"Could be," Wes muttered.

They creaked slowly on under banners stretched from roof to roof. ASPEN WELCOMES THE LITTLE GIANT.

The stores themselves were dark. They'd closed at four o'clock in honor of the event. No building was darker than the Aspen Block, where the parade turned south on Galena.

The upstairs corner office, over the bank, was Bayard's. Ahead of the stage the Flambeau Club was still showering the street with Roman candles. A burst of sparks struck an upper window and brought a gasp from Honora. "I saw a face up there! Pressed against the glass, looking out. Frank Bayard's!"

"Are you sure?" Busy with the reins, Wes hadn't seen it.

"I'm positive. Why is he there? Alone in his dark office?"

Except for a shower of sparks she wouldn't have seen him at all. Wes pondered it as he turned the corner and drove up Galena. "If he was at work there, he'd light the office. And I don't think he's hiding. He could pick a better place to hide. His office is about the first place people would look."

"Then why is he there?" Honora wondered. "Tonight of all nights?"

The parade turned west on Cooper and passed the Brick Saloon. "Only thing I can figure," Wes said, "is that he's there to meet somebody. A sneak meeting or he wouldn't keep the office dark. We got a sneak needs accountin' for, too. Gus Gleason."

Honora thought of Harv Random's theory — that Gleason knew the truth about Bayard's fraud. Gleason was Mr. UT — the killer of John Hostetter and the would-be killer of Wes Brian.

From the sidewalk Colonel Rolfe Clemson waved to Wes, tipped his hat to Honora. Both were too absorbed to see him. "Let's shoot from another angle," Wes pondered. "Say Gleason's in it for a split. He's been jumpy ever since we saw him at a window. He gets jumpier when you and Harv leave town. He gets still jumpier when he sees you and Harv and me get off the train tonight. He thinks maybe we've got the goods on Bayard. After we spill it he'll never collect a cent. So he puts on pressure to force a quick pay-off."

"You mean tonight? At Bayard's office?"

"That's where Bayard's waiting, isn't it? In the dark? What else is he there for?"

At Mill the column turned south to the Clarendon.

Committeemen on the walk helped the governor out. "Banquet's at ten, Governor. Gives you half an hour to rest."

Harv and Waring came along with Roger Norman. Harv handed Honora down and she linked arms with her father. After a few excited words with him, she turned to smile up at Wes Brian.

But Wes wasn't there. He'd jumped to the ground and tossed the reins to Harv. "Put the outfit away, will you, Harv? Or turn it over to Carson. I got some unfinished business."

He was off at a run, disappearing down Mill Street.

234

At Hyman he turned east to the Aspen Block and stopped there, looking up at windows over the bank. The shades were down. But Bayard's private office at the front, Wes thought, was lighted back of the shade. It meant Bayard was still there.

He'd kept the office dark while the parade passed. Now the street was quiet and empty. The crowd had followed the parade or gone home or to the Cooper Avenue bars, some surging toward the Rink Opera House where there'd be a banquet at ten. With the street empty, Bayard might lower the shade and turn on a light.

Wes went up the dark steps, letting his boot heels click. *If he hears me, he'll think I'm Gleason.*

In the gloom of the upper hall Wes had to grope for the right door. It opened into Bayard's reception office and as expected he found it unlighted. But an inner door to the private office had frosted glass. A brightness there told of a glow beyond it.

Suddenly the glass went black. The inner office light had been turned off!

It made Wes cautious. Something wasn't quite right. In some way he'd miscalculated. He stood still for a moment, thinking, midway between Honora's desk and the safe.

He heard me coming. If he thinks I'm Gleason, and if he's waiting for Gleason, would he turn off the light?

Wes took a wary step to the left, bumped into the safe's open door. Only Bayard could have opened the safe. He wouldn't leave without locking it. So he was still here. Why had he opened it tonight? Was it to get a pay-off for Gleason?

He knows I'm out here. Does he know I'm not Gleason?

He'd know it if Gleason had come and gone. He'd know it if Gleason was in there now!

Drawing his gun, Wes advanced softly toward the inner door.

Halfway to it he stopped again, his wits sparking. When the parade passed, the office was dark. Later it was lighted, shades drawn. Now it was dark again. Gleason, arriving since the parade, might find Bayard waiting in the dark. Suppose Bayard handed him a money bag! Gleason would open it to count the money. To count money he'd need a light. But at the sound of footsteps he'd darken the office again.

"Are you in there, Bayard?"

There was no answer.

"Why don't you jump out the window? Afraid you'll break a leg?"

There was no sound of an opening window.

"Anybody with you, Bayard?" Wes expected no answer, got none. He still wasn't sure whether Bayard was alone in there.

He moved forward till his outstretched hand touched the partition. Groping along it he came to the door. His hand slid down frosted glass to a knob.

Wes twisted the knob. As he pushed the door inward he dropped flat on his chest. A gun roared from the private office. Its bullet came through the open doorway and clanged against the safe. In the flash Wes glimpsed two men. One was standing, one was sitting. The standing man, Gleason, had a bag in one hand and a gun in the other. The sitting man was slumped forward, motionless, over a desk.

Gleason's gun boomed again and again his bullet went heart-high over Wes. Wes, prone in the doorway, aimed at the flash and fired.

He heard Gleason stumble. The next flash was lower, thigh-high. Gleason was on his knees shooting wildly. The flash showed Bayard again, slumped over the desk. Bayard hadn't moved. Therefore he couldn't move. He was either stunned or dead.

Wes fired again at the flash from Gleason. This time the man fell forward with a heavy thump. For a moment Wes could hear his choked breathing. Then silence. No more shots came. In a little while Wes got to his feet and groped for a light.

When the office was lighted he took one long look at Gleason and another at Frank Bayard. The sign was fairly clear. Bayard had been clubbed with a gun. The gun in Gleason's dead hand had a bloody barrel. The clubbing must have happened since the passing of the parade.

But why? Maybe because the pay-off wasn't enough. A small leather bag lay beside Gleason. Wes knew without looking that money was in it.

Or even if the pay-off was the sum agreed on, Gleason still had reason to kill Bayard. Bayard, and only Bayard, knew for sure that he'd murdered Hostetter. Gleason knew Bayard was a thief; Bayard knew Gleason was a murderer. No wonder Bayard had hired a bodyguard! Until pay-off day he'd been safe from Gleason; so till then he'd let the guard earn his pay by guarding Honora.

Wes rolled a cigaret, sat down to wait. If the shots had been heard he'd soon have company.

Presently footsteps came running up Hyman. Wes opened a window and looked out. "Up here, officers." Patrolmen Webb and Bacon were on the walk below.

They came dashing up.

Patiently Wes told them the story.

"There's a guess or two in it," he finished wearily. "But maybe there won't be after a court looks at the *Lost Friend* stock certificate. Nothing makes sense unless Bayard rubbed out my name. Look, fellas. I was up all last night tradin' bullets with Gil Dillon and the Buford gang. Ask Harv Random about it. Meantime what about lettin' me catch up on sleep?"

Webb looked at Bacon and both men nodded with a grim sympathy. "We'll take over, Wes, if you'll do just one more thing. On your way to bed, stop at the Rink and tell McEvoy he's needed here."

Until he got to the street Wes hadn't realized how tired he was. The siege on Cattle Creek had lasted twenty-eight hours. The train ride and the parade had kept him keyed up. And now this.

But the Rink was only a block out of his way to the Clarendon.

The street in front of it was packed with carriages. The banquet was now well under way with nearly three hundred guests. The biggest names in Colorado were in there.

Haggard and disheveled and gunslung, Wes Brian brushed by the doorman. He saw five long tables decorated with smilax and his eyes searched them for McEvoy. Every seat was occupied — except two. The two, reserved by Bayard for himself and Honora, were only four chairs from the governor.

At the head table Toastmaster Jim Downing stood ruddily between Alva Adams and David Moffat. In his rich courtroom voice Downing finished his speech:

"Then here's to Aspen, her youth and her age,
We welcome the railroad, say farewell to the stage;
And whatever our lot, wherever we be,
Here's God bless forever the D & R G."

In the cheers, Wes caught McEvoy's eye and beckoned.

The marshal had a hundred questions. It was nearly midnight when Wes got away from him. A dragging weariness made him stumble as he went into the Clarendon lobby.

Night Clerk Neal Hutton shook his head sadly. "Sorry, Wes. We're bulging at the seams. Not an empty room in the house."

"Yes there is." Wes held up a room key. "Rufus Drake won't be home tonight. He loaned me his bed."

As he climbed the stairs Wes wished the ceiling wasn't so high. His boots had lead in them. A dim light burned in the upper hall as he passed down it toward Drake's room, Number 28.

Honora hadn't given up her own room and he knew it was 24. Wes had to pass it on the way. Its transom was dark. Not to awaken her he tiptoed by.

At Number 28 he put the key in the lock. Then the door of 24 opened and Honora came toward him along the hall. She was in robe and slippers; her dark red hair, down for the night, fell loose over her shoulders. She must have been watching at her window as he'd entered from the street.

Wes waited till she came to him. The wonder of it made him humble. "You shouldn't be up, Honora. Go back to bed."

Her lips and her anxious eyes asked the same question. "Was he there?"

"Yes. And Gleason too. They won't trouble us any more."

A little shudder passed through her as she realized what he meant. He drew her to him gently and kissed her. Then the tension dissolved and left her upturned face calm and relaxed. "Now I can sleep! I've been so afraid for you, Wesley dear."

He led her back to her door. "Goodnight, Honora. We'll talk about it tomorrow." But tomorrow was too weak a word. "I mean all the tomorrows — *our* tomorrows clear to the end of the run."

"I'll dream about them," she promised, and was gone.

He stood for a little while outside her door and all the tiredness went away.

240